Other titles by

RACHEL LINDSAY
IN HARLEQUIN PRESENTS

Other titles by

RACHEL LINDSAY
IN HARLEQUIN ROMANCES

Many of these titles, and other titles in the Harlequin
Romance series, are available at your local
bookseller or through the Harlequin Reader Service.
For a free catalogue listing all available Harlequin
Presents and Harlequin Romances, send your name
and address to:

HARLEQUIN READER SERVICE,
M.P.O. Box 707
Niagara Falls, N.Y. 14302
Canadian address
Stratford, Ontario, Canada N5A 6W4.
or use order coupon at back of books.

RACHEL LINDSAY

affair in venice

Harlequin Books

TORONTO • LONDON • NEW YORK • AMSTERDAM • SYDNEY

Harlequin Presents edition published August 1975
ISBN 0-373-70604-9

Second printing December 1976
Third printing March 1977

Original hardcover edition published in 1975
by Mills & Boon Limited

CHAPTER ONE

ERICA RAYBURN looked at the diamond ring winking on her finger and wondered how it would feel to own a three-thousand-pound bauble. Slipping it off, she returned it to its black velvet bed and put it under the glass counter, snapping the lock shut as she did so.

Despite working for six months in the luxury atmosphere of Botelli's, one of Venice's most illustrious jewellery shops, she was still awestruck by the exquisite jewels surrounding her, each one costing more than she earned in a year. Surprisingly for someone who catered for an élite clientele, Signora Botelli herself was a practical, motherly Italian who regarded all her clients as friends, and all the people who worked for her as her protegées. Erica still found it difficult to believe her luck in getting the opportunity to work for her, since she had no practical qualifications other than a deep love of precious stones and antique jewellery, and a gifted amateur's ability to design and make pieces herself.

'Loving the things you sell is halfway to being a good saleswoman,' the Signora had said when she engaged Erica. 'Most girls of your age see the jewellery here as portable bank accounts. But you enjoy each piece because of the care that went into its making.'

'I appreciate its value too,' Erica had protested, not wishing to be thought as unworldly as the Signora made out. But the woman had refused to be dissuaded from her viewpoint, and still held it after knowing Erica for six months.

This belief in her assistant's ingenuousness stemmed, Erica knew, from the aura of simplicity which not even skilful make-up and an austere hair-style could eradicate. Indeed, the more sophisticated she tried to look, the less she succeeded, so that now she accepted the fact that she looked five years younger than the twenty-three she was, and considerably more innocent than she felt herself to be. Not that she was worldly when compared with the bored beauties who made up a large part of their clientele. One in particular came into her mind: a husky-voiced young widow who, for the last three months, had been a consistent buyer of small but expensive items with which to adorn herself. Not that Claudia Medina's beauty required any adornment. She was so lovely that it was a wonder she had not yet married again. There was no doubt the choice would be hers. Sighing for the fact that she herself did not have a matt olive skin and mahogany red hair, Erica took out a pendant from the glass case and started to polish it.

It was a quiet time of the day. She had re-opened the shop after the usual two-hour lunch break and most of the tourists were not yet in evidence, it being both too early in the season and too early in the afternoon. It was the time of year Erica liked best. Spring had not quite given way to summer, and though the chilly morning and evening mists had gone, the city still had the fresh, dew-like quality one seemed to find nowhere else except in Venice.

Venice. City of bridges and slow-moving canals; of narrow winding streets and breathtakingly beautiful squares; of magnificent crumbling palazzos and damp-ridden tenements.

The buzz of the bell above the door brought her back to her present surroundings and she saw a young, pretty girl standing by the counter. Before Erica had a chance to speak, the girl opened her handbag and, rummaging among a conglomeration of coins, gold-backed comb, small calf diary and purse, withdrew a brooch.

'I'd like to sell this,' she said in a breathless voice.

Erica examined the brooch carefully. It was an exquisite thing in gold and rubies, with a large and unusual pink stone in the centre. It was so pale a pink that it reminded her of a dawn sky, though it glittered with the brilliance of a light.

'How much will you give me for it?' the girl asked, still speaking Italian.

Erica hesitated. As a general rule Signora Botelli did not buy second-hand jewellery, though there were times when – in order to help a client who needed some ready cash – she would buy back some of her own work. But this brooch, Erica surmised, had not been produced by any of the craftsmen the Signora employed. It had the patina of age; the stamp of antiquity that would increase its value and make it difficult for her to assess its worth.

'I would like Signora Botelli to see it,' she murmured. 'Perhaps you could call back at five o'clock.'

'I can't. It was difficult enough for me to get away now, without having to—' The girl stopped abruptly, as if afraid she had said too much. 'I'll take a half million lire,' she finished. 'It is worth at least treble that.'

It probably was, Erica decided, and wondered why the girl wanted to sell it and, even more important, if it was hers to sell. A surreptitious but careful glance showed her to be wearing a simple but expensive suit in hand-woven wool. Her handbag was equally expensive, its soft calf exactly matching the hand-stitched gloves which had been carelessly dropped on to the counter. Whatever else she might be, the girl was not a maid who had stolen her mistress's jewellery; yet neither was she a *demi-mondaine* trying to cash in on a present she had received.

'I am afraid you will have to come back and see Signora Botelli,' Erica reiterated. 'I cannot make an offer for the brooch myself.'

'Then what's the point of your being here? If you can't make decisions you might as well close the shop!'

'I can sell,' Erica replied with a faint smile. 'But I am not allowed to buy.'

The girl's pert features were marred by a scowl. It put a line on the smooth forehead and a shadow in the blue eyes.

'If you really can't come back,' Erica continued tentatively, 'there are several other shops who might be interested in the brooch. Carema are always looking for good pieces and—'

'I know where to go,' the girl interrupted rudely. 'That's why I came here. I want to sell this brooch quietly – without any fuss – and Carema know my – know my—' She hesitated and frowned.

Erica was more than ever convinced the girl was trying to surreptitiously dispose of a gift. But it was more than she dared do to buy it. She picked it up and regretfully held it out. It really was one of the loveliest pieces she had seen. 'I'm terribly sorry I can't make you an offer, *signorina*. But as I said, if you return later this afternoon . . .'

The girl glanced out of the window at the crowds strolling in the direction of San Marco Square. A group of Italian women came towards the shop and she gave a gasp and stepped back, as if afraid of being seen. 'I can't return this afternoon,' she muttered, 'but I can probably come back in the morning. Will Signora Botelli be here then?'

'I'll make sure that she is. If you could tell me what time we can expect you?'

'As near to ten as I can make it.' Hurriedly the girl picked up her gloves and went to the door.

'You have forgotten the brooch,' Erica called.

'Keep it for me.'

'But—'

'You look honest,' the girl said, and quickly closed the door behind her.

Erica picked up the brooch and studied it. How trusting of the girl to leave it here: she had not even bothered to get a receipt. But then she had obviously been in a hurry to get away. Erica glanced through the window at the group who had attracted the girl's attention, but they had disappeared. Quickly she put the brooch into a velvet-lined drawer, then resumed cleaning the pendant.

There were few visitors to the shop during the afternoon, apart from some Americans who were more interested in looking than buying, and an old client who returned a ring to be reset, which Erica promised to do herself, since she knew the woman wanted to wear it the following day.

'I thought one needed to be strong to be a jeweller,' the woman commented, looking at Erica's fine-boned wrists.

'Dexterity and patience are more important than strength,' Erica smiled. 'Don't worry, *signora*, re-setting the ring won't be difficult. I'll have it ready for you this time tomorrow.'

She had just put the ring on her work bench when her employer walked in. Signora Botelli was almost as wide as she was tall, with a pair of shrewd black eyes set in a full moon face. But she had the small, beautiful feet and ankles of the true northern Italian, and still walked with a grace that was surprising in one so heavy.

'Sorry to be late,' she puffed. 'But it's becoming more and more difficult to get people to keep their word on delivery. If I don't have better luck before the end of the week, I will have to buy some stock from Rome.'

'You hate paying Roman prices,' Erica reminded her.

'I know. But I can't have an empty window.'

'At least I can offer you one beautiful piece to put in it.' Erica opened the drawer and took out the brooch left in her care by the unknown girl.

Signora Botelli pounced on it. 'Where did you get this?'

Erica explained as her employer examined the brooch carefully.

'You say she wants half a million lire for it?' the woman questioned.

'Yes. You might be able to get it for less. I think she is anxious to make a quiet sale.'

'I don't doubt it,' Signora Botelli remarked caustically. 'Especially if this brooch is the one I think it is.'

Knowing there was significance behind the words,

9

Erica waited. She did not have to wait long, for her employer went into the inner office and returned with a large, well-thumbed book. It was the Bible of the jewellery trade and showed some of the greatest collections in the world, both private ones and museum-owned. A pudgy finger moved down the index, pages were quickly turned and there was a sharp exclamation.

'There!' said the Signora, and held the book under Erica's nose. 'Half a million, did you say? Ten million, more likely!'

Erica stared at a colour reproduction of the brooch. 'The Rosetti Rose,' she read aloud, 'so called because of the rare pink diamond in its centre.'

Taking the book in her hand she read on. The brooch was part of the famous Rosetti Collection and belonged to the family of that name. It had been made for a Countess Rosetti in the seventeenth century and the pink diamond was reputed to have been given to her by an eminent Roman cardinal.

Erica looked at the Signora. 'I can't believe the girl stole it. She didn't look like a thief.'

'Thieves usually don't,' the Signora replied.

'But she looked so—' Erica's arched brows drew together in a frown, 'so well cared for. I *can't* believe she stole it.'

'I'm sure the Conte Rosetti didn't give it to her to sell!'

'You mean the Rosetti family still exists?'

'*Si, si.* They are extremely well known. One of the wealthiest families in Italy – in Europe. It is inconceivable they would sell any of their heirlooms.'

'Perhaps the girl is his wife?'

'The Conte isn't married.'

'His girl-friend, then?'

'No, no,' the Signora said. 'He is not the sort of man to give family jewels to a mistress.'

'You speak as if you know him.'

'I do not know him personally, but I am well acquainted with his character. We will have to telephone him and let him know we have the brooch.'

'Are you sure it's the Rosetti Rose and not a copy?'

'This pink diamond is genuine,' came the firm reply. 'And there is only one like it in the world. I will telephone and make an appointment to see him.'

The Signora disappeared into the office again, returning a moment later to say that the Conte was in Rome and would not be back until the evening. 'I didn't want to leave my name,' she went on, 'in case someone in his household got to hear of it.'

'Does that mean you think one of his servants might have stolen it?'

'It is the only possible solution.' The Signora picked up the brooch and with a faint sigh put it into a small safe where their more expensive items were kept.

'What happens when the girl comes back in the morning?' Erica asked.

'That depends what Conte Rosetti wants to do. He is paranoically adverse to publicity, so we dare not call in the police without his permission.' The black eyes were sharp. 'Did the girl say what time she would be coming in?'

'About ten.'

'Then I will call the Conte at nine-thirty. That should give him time to decide what to do.'

The arrival of a group of tourists – recommended by the concierge from a five-star hotel – prevented any further discussion of the matter. It was well after seven o'clock before they left, and half past before the Signora was ready to lock up the shop.

Despite a two-hour luncheon break, the working hours were long, and Erica felt more than usually tired as she bade her employer goodnight. Perhaps learning that the girl she had seen earlier that day was a thief had depressed her – as knowledge of human fallibility was apt to do – but whatever the reason for it, it lay upon her like a cloud, spoiling her appreciation of the blue dusk that was settling on the city; a time of day which she invariably enjoyed more than any other.

Slowly she skirted the square and walked past the side of San Marco church to the narrow cobbled street that led to the apartment she rented. It was in a shabby old building and gave her no view other than a glimpse of a canal, though even this required her to lean as far out of her bedroom window as safety allowed. But despite being small and viewless it was fairly quiet; a benefit not to be overlooked in Italy, where noise was regarded as a sign of happiness.

To combat her mood, Erica decided to treat herself to dinner in one of the many cafés to be found off the main tourist section. Here the Venetians themselves were catered for, and though the décor was generally simple, with plastic-topped tables and utilitarian steel cutlery, the food was as bountiful – and frequently as good – as one could get at the big hotels and, Erica knew, considerably cheaper.

Tonight she made for a little restaurant a couple of blocks from where she lived. Recognizing her as she came in – for she was a regular weekly visitor – the *patron* came over with a glass and a half bottle of Chianti, and stood beaming down at her while she looked at the menu and toyed between a choice of *fritto misto* – a delicious assortment of small fish fried to a crisp in oil – or *osso bucco*: veal shanks cooked in a sauce of fresh tomatoes, white wine and rosemary.

'I'll have the *osso bucco*, I think,' she said.

'A little pasta to begin with?'

She shook her head. 'Think of my figure, *signore!*'

'I do,' he chuckled. 'All the time!'

She laughed, too used to his flirtatious ways to be embarrassed by them. 'Just the *osso bucco*,' she reiterated.

As she waited for her meal to arrive she sipped her wine and slowly relaxed, thinking again of the rose diamond brooch. It was hard to believe that the girl who had brought it in was a thief. It was all very well for Signora Botelli to say thieves did not give themselves away, but the girl had possessed an indefinable air of breeding that had not come from acting ability. She had looked as though the brooch

12

was hers; as if she had the right to possess it. So intently was Erica concentrating on the happenings of that afternoon that she only became aware of being watched when she finally looked round to signal the proprietor for her bill.

'You will allow me to buy you a drink?' said the young man at the next table.

'No, thank you,' she smiled. 'I am leaving.'

'But the night is young. Please let me persuade you to change your mind?'

Erica shook her head, glad her apartment was only a few doors away. If living in Italy had any disadvantage, it was the young Italian males. They were notoriously persistent suitors and would frequently pester an unescorted girl to the point of becoming a nuisance.

'I prefer my own company, *signore*, but thank you for your offer.'

The liquid brown eyes were reproachful. 'It is too lovely a night for a beautiful girl to be alone.'

'Not if she prefers it that way.' Thankfully Erica turned to accept her bill, and she went over to the counter to pay it, resolutely refusing to look behind her in case her admirer took it as a sign that she was relenting.

'You have problems?' the *patron* murmured as he gave her some change.

'Not unless the young man follows me.'

'I will make sure he doesn't. Go quickly while I stand in the doorway and watch until you reach your apartment.'

Thanking him for his kindness, she hurried out before the arrival of any new customers made it difficult for him to keep his promise, and only as she reached her own front door and closed it behind her did she allow herself to relax.

Dropping her jacket on to a chair, she kicked off her shoes and padded over to switch on the radio. As always there was opera music to be found, and humming her own accompaniment to a Rossini overture, she set about making herself some coffee.

Mug in hand, she settled into the only easy chair the room had, and glanced at the airmail edition of *The Times*. It was the one link with England that she refused to give up, even though she sometimes felt it to be an unnecessary expense. But reading about the latest British crisis or trying to do the impossible clues in the crossword puzzle satisfied the homesickness that often encompassed her at this time of the evening. No matter how long she lived abroad, she doubted if she would ever feel anything other than English; nor could she be mistaken for anything else either, for she had the colouring of a true Anglo-Saxon: skin the colour of a creamy tea rose, unusually large, dark grey eyes and silky hair that looked either silvery beige or pale blonde according to the time of day. At the moment it looked silvery beige, which made her skin seem paler too. Turning her head, she studied her image in the ornate Venetian mirror that covered nearly the whole of one wall. It was the only unusual feature in an otherwise ordinary room, and had been her most extravagant purchase to date. How she would manage to take it back with her to England she did not know. But time enough to worry about that when she left. She finished her coffee and stood up, a slender girl whose greyhound grace was emphasized by her quick, light movements. Compared with the somewhat overblown Italian women Erica felt herself to be very much understated, and often wished she were more positive-looking, failing to see the charm of her porcelain colouring and cameo-like features.

The chiming of a clock in the distance made her aware of the lateness of the hour, and she undressed and climbed into bed. In another month the heat of the city would be stifling, and she hoped she had the stamina to see the season through. It would be her first one here and she did not want to let down the Signora. Heaven knew where she would find another job as interesting as this one. It was not simply that she loved the beauty of Venice or enjoyed working in the shop, but that she was being allowed to design her own jewellery and given the opportunity to study the works of some of the brilliant craftsmen whom the Signora employed. Erica's fortnightly visit to the Botelli workshop on the outskirts of the city was the highlight of her existence, though she knew that the peak would be achieved when the necklace she was now working on was displayed for sale in the window. Yet how laborious her design was when compared with the superb workmanship of the Rosetti Rose. It had been singularly stupid of her not to have recognized its value when she had first seen it.

She sighed and hoped that the Conte's dislike of publicity would allow him to let the thief go unprosecuted. Such a pretty creature would not have resorted to stealing unless she was in great trouble.

CHAPTER TWO

ERICA overslept next morning, and because she did not like being late she rushed from her apartment without breakfast.

The day was sunny and had brought out slowly ambling Americans and groups of black-haired Japanese men all busy clicking their cameras. Because of this it was difficult to make fast progress through the streets, and it was well after half past nine before she reached the shop and slid back the iron gate from the window.

Luckily there was no sign of her employer, and she wondered if the woman had gone directly to seek the Conte. Yet she could not have done so, for the brooch was still in the safe. She had noticed it when she had taken out some rings – the more valuable ones were placed there each night – to put back in the window.

Going into the small office, she took out the gold necklace she was in the middle of making. Simultaneously the bell above the door chimed and she swung back into the shop as a man walked in. Yet walk was an inadequate verb to describe the way he moved; he seemed to glide in, dwarfing the small interior with his height and diminishing the splendour around him with his incredibly handsome face. He was, without doubt, the most striking-looking man she had ever seen. His olive skin and satin-black hair proclaimed him a Mediterranean, though he had the narrow features of a Spaniard: longish nose, thin but well defined mouth and heavy-lidded, sloe-shaped dark eyes. But when he spoke his Italian was faultless, as was the navy silk suit he wore, its impeccable cut drawing attention to his wide shoulders and lean hips. His manner was as crisp as his linen and equally starchy.

'Signora Botelli?'

'She has not yet arrived. I am her assistant. May I

help you—'

He ignored the offer. 'What time will she be here?'

'I am expecting her at any moment. May I help you?' Erica said again.

His lower lip jutted forward as if he were thinking. 'You work here the whole time?' he asked suddenly.

'Yes.'

'You were here yesterday?'

'I am here every day.'

'I am concerned with yesterday afternoon. Were you here then?'

Erica nodded. 'Signora Botelli was out most of the afternoon, but I was here the whole time.'

She glanced at him and saw he was frowning. Could his wife have bought something here that he did not like or which he found too expensive? Somehow she did not think expense would matter to him, though she had no doubt that he had strong likes and dislikes.

'If you have come about a piece of jewellery . . .' she murmured.

'Indeed I have. A gold brooch with a pink diamond in the centre.' Correctly reading Erica's astonished expression, his own became more aloof. 'You appear to know the brooch I mean?'

'I do. A young girl brought it in yesterday. She wanted to sell it.'

'And you offered her half a million lire for it?'

'Oh no,' Erica corrected, and looked over the man's shoulder at the door, hoping that her employer would not be long in coming through it. Was this man the girl's accomplice come to demand either payment for the brooch or its return? Yet she dared not give it back to him in case he disappeared with it; nor would she give him the money. She moistened her lips and tried not to show her nervousness.

'I was under the impression that you offered to pay half a million lire,' he repeated, his voice menacing.

'I most certainly didn't,' Erica said firmly. 'The girl said she would be willing to *take* that amount, but I told her I couldn't buy it without my employer's approval.'

'But you kept the brooch, didn't you? You made sure of that!'

'The girl insisted on leaving it here. I didn't ask her to do so.'

'Then you will kindly give it back to me.'

Erica drew a deep breath. 'I'm afraid I can't.'

His eyes glittered. 'You mean you haven't got it?'

'Of course I've got it – it's in the safe – but I can't give it to you.'

'We'll see about that!' His voice was harsh. 'Were it not for the scandal, I would report you immediately to the police!'

'I haven't done anything wrong, *signore*,' she cried, and was annoyed to feel her face flame with colour. That he had noticed it she could tell from the angry gleam in his eyes as he came a step closer.

'You hardly look the picture of innocence,' he said crisply. 'You've flamed up like a peony.'

'Because I find you extremely intimidating.'

'Then give me the brooch and I will go.'

'You will have to wait for Signora Botelli. I expected her at half past nine, but – but I think she must have gone to an appointment first.'

'I have no intention of waiting for the Signora's return.' The man made an effort to control his temper. 'Will you please be kind enough to return my brooch to me and count yourself lucky that I will take the matter no further.'

'*Your* brooch?' she gasped.

'Mine,' he repeated. 'Give it to me at once.'

Erica moistened her lips. 'Are you . . . Do you mean you are . . .'

'The Conte Filippo Rosetti.' There was no expression in his voice. 'The brooch you considered yourself so lucky to obtain is *my* property. If you doubt my credentials—' With a flourish he withdrew his wallet and flicked it open to show her his driving licence.

'Please,' she protested. 'There's no need to give me proof.

I believe you.'

'Then let me have the brooch and be done with it. I have wasted enough time here already.'

This was more than plain speaking; it was downright uncivil, and Erica's temper, normally slow to rise, began to do so. 'I have already told you that I can't give you the brooch until my employer arrives. I'm sure she'll be here soon.'

His brows drew together, forming a thick black line above his eyes. 'It is a pity you didn't show as much care in taking the brooch as you do in returning it. Or do you frequently buy stolen property? I believe it can often be obtained at an advantageous price.'

'You have no right to say a thing like that!'

'I have every right. You take possession of an extremely valuable heirloom – offer a pittance for it knowing full well it is not legitimately on the market – and then you have the audacity to question my right to have it returned to me!'

'I'm not questioning your right,' she said passionately. 'I'm merely telling you that I must wait until my employer gets here. I would also like to inform you that I had no idea it was an heirloom nor that it was so valuable.'

'Don't you know anything about jewellery?'

'Of course I do.'

'Then how can you say you didn't know its worth?'

Irritated at being disbelieved, she snapped: 'One doesn't usually get the chance of seeing such a piece; and the Rosetti Rose isn't so well known that I'd be likely to recognize it. I'm an ordinary jeweller, *signore*, not a dealer in antiquities!'

'Even an ordinary jeweller,' he said scathingly, 'would know the value of a pink diamond.'

'Well, I didn't.'

'Then you should be selling bonbons, *signorina!*'

His rudeness took her breath away, which was a good thing, for she might have said something she would afterwards have regretted. Before she could find her breath again, Signora Botelli walked in.

With a swiftness that put Erica to shame she immediately

recognized the man. 'Conte Rosetti,' she said graciously. 'Only a few moments ago I was speaking to your secretary. He said you were out and I left my name. I did not expect you to get here so quickly.'

'I received no message from you, *signora*.' The man's temper was replaced by icy calm. 'I learned the whereabouts of my brooch late last night – unfortunately too late for me to contact you – which is why I came here first thing this morning. If you would be kind enough to return it to me, I will consider the matter closed.'

The Signora looked nonplussed, as well she might, for there was nothing in the Conte's manner to show he was pleased to have his brooch back. Rather he conveyed the impression that in accepting it without recourse to the police, he was doing them a favour.

'The Conte believes we knew the brooch had been stolen and that we offered to buy it for half a million lire,' Erica explained to her employer. 'I hope you can disabuse him of that idea. I'm afraid I haven't been able to do so.'

Every inch of the Signora's massive frame quivered with indignation and she looked like a jelly on the boil. 'If I wish to buy your brooch, Conte Rosetti, I would not have telephoned your home last night nor again this morning.'

'Then why did you accept the brooch in the first place?'

'*I* was the one who accepted it,' Erica intervened angrily. 'And I have already told you I did not recognize it.'

'My assistant is speaking the truth,' Signora Botelli confirmed. 'A young girl brought it in and insisted on leaving it here. She was willing to sell it for half a million lire, but my assistant has no authority to buy any jewellery and she asked the girl to return this morning.'

'Which she was supposed to do at ten o'clock,' Erica spoke again.

'I am here in her place.' The man ignored Erica and looked at the Signora. 'Please let me have it and the matter can be forgotten.'

'Of course you can have the brooch.' The Signora went to

the safe. 'But I must insist that you apologize to us. My reputation does not warrant your attack on it.'

There was silence in the little shop and Erica held her breath. From the paleness of the Conte's face she could tell he was not normally given to apologizing; either because he believed he was never wrong or because even if he were, no one had yet had the temerity to tell him so. Yet here was the plump Signora not only telling him he had made a mistake but demanding an apology for it!

'You are quite correct, *signora*. I had no right to jump to such a conclusion. Please forgive me.'

Erica heard the apology with astonishment. Was this the Conte's voice, this gentle, almost kindly tone that bore no relation to the frigid one of a moment ago?

'My only excuse,' he went on, 'is that personal matters have made it hard for me to maintain my usual calm and logic. Had I not been distressed, I would have known better than to impugn a reputation which – as you well know – is recognized to be the highest in the city. Again I beg you to forgive me.'

He paused and Erica waited, not sure if he was going to suggest buying something expensive as a further sop to Signora Botelli's anger. But he was far too intelligent to be so obvious. Instead he bestowed a smile of singular sweetness on them both, making Erica realize once more that she was standing in front of the most handsome man she had ever seen. If the Conte epitomized Italian masculinity – and coming from such lineage he probably did – small wonder that the marble men hewn by Michelangelo should be such magnificent specimens of virile strength and beauty. The last word caught at her imagination, for it was rare that one could apply it to a man. Yet it fitted this one. Beauty without a hint of feminity; virility and assurance so well tempered that, like the finest steel, its strength could only be guessed at.

The Signora took the Rosetti Rose from the safe, but as she went to place it in a box the Conte reached out and put it unceremoniously into his pocket.

'Be careful,' Erica said before she could stop herself.

He looked at her. With anger no longer darkening his eyes, she saw they were not black as she had supposed, but dark brown and fringed by incredibly thick lashes.

'The brooch has had far worse treatment than being placed unwrapped in a pocket, *signorina*.'

His smile revealed perfect white teeth, and crossly she wondered if there was anything to fault about this man or if everything about him was perfect. At least she could object to his manner without feeling she was deliberately looking for a flaw. Not even his apology – charming though it was – could make her forget the quick way he had assumed she had tried to buy the brooch knowing it was stolen: that she had actually used this knowledge to try and obtain it at a ridiculously low price.

'You look as if you do not believe me?' The Conte spoke again and she knew he had misread her expression, assuming it to be doubt of his last remark rather than dislike of his behaviour. 'I can assure you this brooch has received much harsh treatment. The Contessa for whom it was made was famous for her rages. Many times she took off the brooch and flung it at the cause of her bad temper. The first time it hit the face of the cardinal who had had it made for her – and drew his blood – and the next was when she flung it at the girl who had seduced her husband.'

'It's usually the man who seduces,' Erica said shortly, determined not to be humoured so easily.

'That is a fallacy encouraged by women! When a man strays, it is generally because a woman entices him.'

'We must agree to differ on that point,' she retorted, and went into the tiny office. Behind her she heard the man speak to the Signora, though his voice was too low for her to make out what he said. It was several moments before the door of the shop closed, and when it did the Signora immediately came into the office.

'Aye! What a piece of luck that the brooch was stolen!'

'I don't see how.'

'It brought him to the shop, didn't it? Now he has seen for

himself the jewellery that we make.'

'With pieces like the Rosetti Rose,' Erica said crisply, 'I can't see him collecting modern stuff.'

'He doesn't collect it,' the Signora smiled. 'He gives it away.'

'To whom?'

'His current mistress.' The fat shoulders lifted. 'Madame Medina at the moment. I thought you knew.'

Erica's smile was rueful. 'There's a great deal going on that I don't know. I suppose I'm more interested in Venice's painted frescoes than its painted women!'

The Signora chuckled. 'Painted women! What an old-fashioned expression. It is not only your father who is living in ancient times.'

Erica grinned. Her father was Professor of Archaeology at a university in England and she was well aware that a great deal of her attitude bore resemblance to his own.

'Does the Conte have many affairs?' she asked carefully.

'Not more than most men in his position.'

'What does his position have to do with it?'

'My dear child, *that* old-fashioned you cannot be! When a man is as good-looking and rich as he is, he has to fight the women away. It would require the disposition of a monk to remain immune to the flattery he receives.'

'He got none from me,' Erica said coldly.

'So I noticed.' The beady black eyes were appraising. 'You made no effort to hide your dislike. Yet he was very charming to you.'

'Only when he was apologizing. You should have heard how rude he was before you came in.'

'He is a worried man. He told me he has a great problem with his niece.' The Signora lowered her voice as though afraid that even in the empty shop someone might hear her and tell the Conte she was speaking of his private life. 'The girl is in love with someone totally unsuitable and has threatened to run away with him.'

'Are you talking of the girl who brought the brooch in?'

'Yes. Apparently the Conte allows her to wear some small pieces from his collection. It was a great shock to him to discover she was prepared to sell one of them. Not merely because she could do so with something that did not belong to her, but because the piece itself is an heirloom.'

This at least was an attitude Erica could understand, and it partially lessened her dislike of the man. 'How did he find out about it?' she asked. 'He said he knew before you had called him.'

'He came home last night – earlier than expected – and brought a couple of business colleagues with him. He asked his niece to dine with him and to wear the Rose. When she didn't do so, he—'

'You mean he told her what to wear?'

'Why shouldn't he?'

'I'd like a man telling *me* what to wear!' Erica snorted.

'You probably would.' The Signora deliberately misunderstood Erica's meaning. 'Most women appreciate a masterful man.' Long distant memories of long-distant passions warmed the plump face. 'Especially if the man combines mastery with tenderness.'

'I'm sure the Conte is brimming over with tenderness!'

'You don't think so?' The little eyes were sharp. 'You have a lot to learn, my child.'

'But not from him!' Erica picked up the gold necklace and continued to work on it. 'I'm surprised he told you his niece had taken the brooch. I thought he'd do anything to keep his family name untarnished.'

'He knows that what he has told me will go no further.'

'He is very trusting of a woman's discretion!'

'He knows that if the story of his niece's behaviour leaked out, it could only come from us.'

'Don't worry about *my* discretion,' Erica assured her. 'I've forgotten it already.'

'Good. If he wished, the Conte could do my business a great deal of harm.'

The woman went out, and Erica thought about the Conte Rosetti's niece. She could not help feeling sorry for the girl.

24

It could not be easy to live with an uncle who regarded himself as the arbiter of right and wrong. She was curious to know what had happened to the girl's father and felt a fleeting interest in the unknown young man who had the temerity to court a girl whom the uncle at least felt to be out of his reach. What made the young man unsuitable? His lack of position or his lack of wealth? She felt that the Conte would be more concerned with social standing than money. Irritably she bent over the pendant. The sooner she forgot this whole incident the better.

Three days later Signora Botelli received an invitation to the opening of a modern jewellery exhibition. She would be in Milan at the time and she asked Erica to go in her place.

'In any case, *you* are the expert,' she said. 'You might see something there that will inspire you to design something else for me. I have already had an offer for that necklace of yours. Signor Bruno wants to buy it for his wife. If he pays me the price I have asked, your commission will be enough for you to move into a better apartment.'

She mentioned a sum of money that took Erica's breath away. 'That's far too generous.'

'How foolish of you to say so! If I thought you had sufficient business acumen – or even ambition – I would suggest you start up on your own. But you are the worst thing of all, my dear child, a gifted amateur! If you could, you would give away your fabulous creations and put hard-working people like myself out of business!'

'It would take more than my great production line to do that!' Erica laughed. 'But you are wrong about my lack of ambition. My real trouble is that by the time I finish a piece I can't bear to sell it.'

'Work on several at a time. In that way you will be like a mother with ten children. You will love them all, but you won't miss one if it goes away!'

'Does that apply to men too?' Erica quipped.

'That is a question no moral woman would dare answer!' Signora Botelli chuckled. 'But such a problem will never concern you, I think. You are the type to love only one.'

It was a comment Erica was to remember with bitterness and pain not many months later.

CHAPTER THREE

ERICA went to the Modern Jewellery Exhibition on Saturday afternoon.

In a city that teemed with exhibitions, this one at the Mendoza Gallery had nonetheless received a great deal of praise. Some of the most important modern designs had been gathered together to show new forms of workmanship and a less stylized use of precious and semi-precious stones. It was the latter which were made into the most eye-catching pieces and amethysts, garnets and even pyrites – little chunks of metal that could gleam like gold – were fashioned into brooches, necklaces and a particularly outstanding paperweight. Modern jewellery, so the Mendoza Gallery proclaimed, should not only be used for the admornment of one's person but also of one's home.

The two long rooms in which the exhibition was housed were filled with people, mostly the elite of the city, and Erica was glad she had taken special pains with her appearance. Though a discerning woman would immediately guess that the honey beige suit had been bought off the peg, she knew that an admiring male would only know that the colour of it almost exactly matched her hair and gave a warm glow to her skin. Tall and slender, she looked like a stalk of corn; not that a corn stalk was noticeable when placed in a vase with tiger lilies and roses, which was the best way of describing the bejewelled and scented females chattering round her. Amused by her fanciful imagination, she went to get a better look at a bracelet. As she did so she became aware of a small group coming through from the other room. Recognizing the Conte Rosetti, she stepped back, unwilling for him to see her. But he was totally absorbed with his own party, and his dark head was lowered attentively towards a sad-faced woman in her early forties, who bore such a striking resemblance to the girl who had come into the shop that Erica guessed her to be the Conte's sister. This was confirmed by the sight of the girl herself. She was walking immediately behind them and talking in a bored manner to a young man in his twenties.

Remaining hidden behind a large urn of flowers, Erica watched as the party moved past the displays, the younger man studying each one with such thoroughness that she sensed him to be looking at it from a professional viewpoint. He was either a jeweller or a display artist. At last they reached the far end of the room, and with a feeling of relief Erica stepped out to continue her own tour. As she did so, the group turned from the door as though to look at something they had missed, and in turning, the Conte came face to face with Erica. For a split second he looked at her blankly, then recognition dawned and he gave a slight bow.

'Good afternoon, Miss – er—' he hesitated and she was reluctantly forced to give him her name. 'Miss Rayburn,' he repeated, and turned to introduce her to the rest of his party. 'My sister, Mrs. Charters; my niece Sophia, whom I believe you have already met, and Donald Phillips who is organizing the Rosetti Exhibition in America.'

Erica smiled her way through the introductions, but when she went to move away found her retreat barred by the Conte. Deciding that to try and leave when he did not want her to do so would only make him more obstinate, she turned her attention to the American.

'I wondered why you kept moving round each display case,' she said. 'Was it to see the lighting?'

'Yes. Italians are past-masters when it comes to display.'

'They are good at every kind of design. I've lived here six months and I'm still astonished at their virtuosity.'

'You work in Venice?' He did not hide his surprise, and hearing it, Conte Rosetti intervened.

'Miss Rayburn sells jewellery at Botelli's.'

'I *make* jewellery too,' Erica said, ignoring the Conte and speaking to the American.

'So you are also at the Exhibition as a professional?' Donald Phillips commented.

'Yes. Signora Botelli thought it might give me some inspiration.'

'Do you prefer modern jewellery to antique?' the Conte's sister inquired. Her soft voice gave an impression of nervousness, though it was not apparent in her demeanour, which held all the confidence one would expect from a member of the Rosetti family.

'If I have any preference at all,' Erica replied, 'it is for very old pieces.'

'Then you shouldn't bother coming to this kind of exhibition.' The Conte's niece spoke for the first time, her words and tone distinctly unfriendly. 'If you don't genuinely care for modern jewellery you'll never be good at designing it.'

Erica gave a non-committal murmur and went to move away. But again the Conte forestalled her, putting out a hand to grip her arm.

'Before you go, Miss Rayburn, my niece would like to apologize to you.'

'Would I?' his niece asked.

'Without question, Sophia. You surely haven't forgotten the inconvenience you caused Miss Rayburn when you left her the Rose Diamond to repair?'

'So you are the one who had the brooch?' Donald Phillips exclaimed. 'Conti Rosetti wanted to show it to me the other night and Sophia had to confess she'd taken it to you.'

'Luckily I was able to retrieve it from Miss Rayburn before she'd had a chance to touch it,' the Conte said smoothly. 'Sophia had not realized that to repair a brooch of such antiquity requires particular skill.'

Erica lowered her lids. How cleverly the Conte had explained the disappearance of the brooch to his guest. The only trouble was that in doing so he had made her look over-eager for work and foolish.

'Come now, Sophia,' the Conte continued. 'Apologize to Miss Rayburn for causing her so much trouble.'

Erica's annoyance with the girl lessened at the taunting

cruelty in the Conte's voice. He might be angry with his niece, but there was no reason for him to be so spiteful. After all, she had wanted to sell the brooch in order to run away with the man she loved; not commendable behaviour but at least understandable in one so young.

'There's no need for you to apologize, Miss Charters,' she said swiftly. 'If anyone should do so, it is your uncle.'

The girl looked astonished. 'My uncle?'

'Certainly. For he has taken it for granted that I am incapable of repairing the Rose Diamond!'

'Could you have done it?' Donald Phillips asked.

Discarding her usual modesty, Erica nodded. 'Repairing antique jewellery is my hobby.'

'What exactly needs doing to it?' the Conte inquired, eyes gleaming with malice.

Erica was delighted she had examined the brooch carefully when it had been left with her. If this supercilious man hoped to catch her out, he was in for a surprise. 'The hasp at the back has worn thin,' she explained, 'and the bed of gold on which the rose diamond is lying has partly worn away.'

His mouth twitched. 'You have a sharp eye, Miss Rayburn. You make it sound serious.'

'It *is* serious.'

Sophia giggled, and the look she gave Erica was far more friendly.

Ignoring the sound, the Conte spoke again. 'Perhaps I *will* give you the opportunity of repairing it after all.'

'I would feel happier if you took it to an expert,' Erica said.

'You have just assured Mr. Phillips that you *are* one.'

'*I* know that,' she said gravely, 'but I'm not sure you do.'

This time the twitch of his mouth was unmistakable. 'You have a sharp tongue as well, Miss Rayburn. I must remember to be careful of it.'

'Filippo!'

The exclamation came from behind Erica and caused the Conte to look over her shoulder. He gave a wide smile of greeting as two men advanced towards him, and as he turned to introduce them to his own party, Erica took the opportunity of moving into the next room.

Her meeting with the Conte and his family had left her unexpectedly edgy, and she had to force herself not to look around and see if they had followed her in here. Her second encounter with the man had in no way altered her opinion of him; indeed it had intensified it, for it showed him to be not only overbearing but sarcastic too. She glanced over her shoulder. From where she was standing she had a good view of the entire gallery, and saw that the Rosetti family had gone. Only then did she breathe a sigh of relief and continue her way round the exhibition. Yet she could not concentrate on it, her mind too occupied with thoughts of a man whose self-confidence she would dearly like to shatter. Many women must have come and gone in his life and she wondered if any of them had had the opportunity of piercing his armour of conceit. Somehow she doubted it. He was a law unto himself.

She moved over to another display and her foot trod on something soft. It was a glove and she bent and picked it up. It was of finest calf and looked extremely expensive. There was an attendant in the corner of the room and she gave it to him and walked on.

She was examining a necklace which she personally thought far less well made than the one she herself had just finished, when she became aware that a man had come to stand beside her. Without looking round she knew who it was. No one else exuded that same smell of Havana cigar smoke and subtle blend of after-shave lotion.

'I came to thank you for finding my sister's glove,' the Conte Rosetti murmured.

There was no help for it but to turn and face him. 'I didn't know it was your sister's.'

'So I gather. The attendant said it was given to him by a blonde foreigner.'

'I thought I'd spoken to him in impeccable Italian!'

He smiled, looking instantly relaxed, and she realized

31

this was the first humorous remark she had made to him. But likely to be the last too, for he looked grave again.

'You appear to have a habit of finding things that my family lose, Miss Rayburn. Perhaps I should engage you as duenna to my womenfolk?'

'I am sure *you* are protector enough!'

'I will be needing one myself if you keep attacking me!' His head tilted sideways. 'What have I done to offend you, *signorina*?'

'Nothing,' she said swiftly. 'I'm sorry if my – if you think I've been attacking you. It's just my way of speaking.'

'Now you are lying to me,' he reproached. 'I am certain your usual way of speaking is as gentle and subtle as your appearance.'

The colour came and went in her cheeks and she knew he was aware of it, for he gave a slight smile. 'Come, Miss Rayburn, tell me what I have done to offend you.'

Knowing he was not the sort of man to be put off by prevarication, she said, 'I didn't like being accused of knowingly receiving stolen property.'

'I have already apologized for that mistake. I am sorry you cannot accept it.'

'It didn't feel like a genuine apology.'

His eyes narrowed. 'I never say what I do not mean, Miss Rayburn. As I explained to Signora Botelli, I have been under a great strain recently. I had hoped she would have explained that to you.' He came a step closer. 'What must I do to make you look on me more kindly?'

'Nothing,' she said, and recognizing the effort it must have cost him to be contrite, had no choice but to accept his plea for forgiveness. 'Let's forget it, Conte. I'm sure my ruffled feelings will be smoothed down in time. By next week I will have forgotten the whole thing.'

'Including myself?'

'You're not the sort of man one can easily forget,' she said truthfully. 'But I will remember you with less and less annoyance.'

'I can see I will have to be content with that reply. For

such a gentle-looking creature you have a will of iron!'

Assuming his remark to be one of departure, she bent down to look at the necklace, but the man remained beside her, and she was uncomfortably aware of him. He was taller than any Italian she had met, and looked far more austere than most of his countrymen. His features were less sensuous, but there was no doubting the controlled emotion of the hooded dark eyes and the firmly closed mouth.

'Are you as interested in that necklace as you are pretending to be?' he asked silkily.

She continued to look at it. 'I'm not pretending.'

'You said you preferred antique jewellery.'

'Signora Botelli wishes me to make some modern pieces for her.'

'Ah.' The sound was satisfied. 'Tell me, Miss Rayburn, is it possible to buy any of your work?'

Aware that she could not keep looking at the necklace, she lifted her head. She had not imagined the amusement in Conte Rosetti's voice, for it was borne out by his expression. For some reason best known to himself he was trying to bait her.

'I am completing a necklace at the moment, for which the Signora has already received an offer.'

'But you will be making other pieces?'

'Of course.'

'Then I will arrange to see them.' He paused as if waiting for her to thank him, and when she did not do so, his look became speculative. 'You consider yourself a good designer?'

'I am pleased with what I do,' she said slowly.

'Then you must be good. I do not think you are a person who is easily satisfied.'

Uncertain whether this was a compliment, she hesitated, and with perception he guessed her doubt.

'Unlike most of your sex, Miss Rayburn, you are not fooled by the third-rate merely because it is expensive.'

'I don't think many women are.'

His eyes sparkled. 'You serve them every day!'

Instantly Erica remembered Claudia Medina. Petite, cur-vaceous and startlingly elegant, she was every inch the type to which he was referring, and inconsequentially Erica won-dered if playing the role of mistress disqualified the woman from becoming the Contessa.

'Was it an interesting thought?' he asked. 'The one that is making you smile.'

'It was an unimportant one.'

'Then perhaps I can replace it with something more interesting. If you admire antique jewellery perhaps you would care to prepare some designs for me? I have a few pieces that need re-setting.'

'It would be desecration to break up something that is really old.'

'I do not need to be told that, Miss Rayburn.' Once more he was austere. 'The pieces I have in mind were left to me by an aunt some years ago. The stones are perfect, but they are ruined by the heavy settings. I am sure you can design something more suitable.'

'But you haven't seen my work.'

'You could hardly design anything worse,' he added.

She chuckled. 'That's a dubious compliment. But I'm preparing some sketches for Signora Botelli and I will ask her to show them to you. If they meet with your approval, we can take it from there.'

'In the meantime perhaps you would care to see the Ros-etti Collection in its entirety? It is a chance given to few people. The more important pieces are usually kept in my bank in Rome, but as the jewellery is going on show in Am-erica, it is all being brought to the Palazzo.'

'I'd love to see it.' She was too delighted to pretend other-wise. 'I hope you have it well insured? Forgive me,' she apologized before he could reply. 'I didn't mean to pry, it's just that the thought of so much jewellery in one place gives me the shudders.'

'Me too,' he said sincerely if ungrammatically. 'But at least one recompense will be my ability to show them to you. I will call you if I may and arrange a time.'

A week passed without any word from Filippo Rosetti and Erica presumed he had either forgotten his invitation or regretted it. Either way it was chastening, and with a need to bolster her morale she went shopping during the week-end and spent far more than she should have done on summer clothes.

As always the understated colours were the ones that appealed to her, and encouraged by a fashion-conscious boutique owner, she chose several dresses in subtle coffee, lemon and cream shades.

'Bright colours swamp you,' the woman had assured her. 'The secret of looking beautiful is—'

'Being beautiful,' Erica interposed.

'No, no, *signorina*, that is where women make a mistake. To *appear* beautiful is to be beautiful. And that means making the best of what you have.'

'I'll have to learn how to do that,' Erica smiled.

'You don't need to try,' the woman assured her. 'With your looks and figure and my clothes, you are already there!'

The admiring male glances that followed her to work on Monday morning in one of her new dresses decided Erica that perhaps the boutique owner had not been flattering her after all. Six months of living alone in this enchanted city had done more than give her a linguistic ability; it had also given her a confidence which had increased her poise and allowed her personality to blossom. Living with her father in a small university town she had been swamped by his life style and needs, and because she loved him, she had put these before her own. Her work as a jeweller had not helped her to escape from the onerous duties of being an only child to a widowed father, for she had learned her craft at the excellent night school which the town boasted, and had then gone on to work part-time in an old-fashioned jewellery shop in the town centre. This had given her some earning power, but had not helped her to lead her own life.

She had met Signora Botelli by chance. The woman's nephew was studying archaeology with Erica's father and halfway through his second term his aunt – in London on

35

business – travelled north to see him. Her delighted nephew had brought her to meet his professor and daughter, and from this had sprung the offer for Erica to work in the Signora's Venice shop and study the Venetian craftsmen.

At first Erica had refused, unable to see how her father could manage without her. But his reaction to this had been surprisingly angry.

'I'm not a child, Erica. I can manage perfectly well on my own. If I hadn't been such a selfish man I would have sent you packing long ago, instead of letting you keep house for me.'

'I'm quite happy staying here,' Erica had assured him. 'I've been toying with the idea of renting a stall in the antique market and—'

'Designing copper necklaces for arty women? Rubbish!'

Rarely had she known her father so vehement, but it was a vehemence which led her to accept the Signora's offer, though she made it clear that she must be free to leave at a moment's notice should her father need her back.

Four months after arriving in Venice, Professor Rayburn married a visiting American archaeologist attached to the university for a sabbatical year. Erica had met her when she had flown back to England for the wedding, and had returned to Venice reassured by the knowledge that her father was no longer a responsibility, though saddened by the fact that she must now make her own life alone.

Signora Botelli's suggestion that she use the extra commission she earned from the sale of her necklace to move into a better apartment was something she had carefully considered. Yet it seemed pointless to waste her money on bigger rooms in a better position. No matter how happy she was in Venice, she could not envisage living here permanently – certainly not if she remained single – for the life of a middle-aged spinster in an Italian town had little to commend it. At least in England there were social clubs, evening classes and a host of concerts and lectures one could attend alone. But Italy was still a patriarchal society, where

36

women were regarded as second-class citizens, and where those unlucky enough to remain unmarried and without families to whom they could devote themselves were treated with even less consideration. At twenty-three it was easy for her to enjoy her life here, but it would be unwise to consider it as permanent.

She skirted San Marco Square enjoying, as she always did, her brief glimpse of it, and turned down the narrow street that led to the shop. As she unlocked the front door she saw a large silver-grey envelope on the mat. Her name was typed on it, and assuming it to be another invitation to an exhibition, she opened it.

Expecting the card inside to be printed, she was surprised to see firm black writing. At once she knew it was from the Conte Rosetti. Quickly she read it: it was an invitation to lunch with him next Sunday and apologized for not having been in touch with her earlier, explaining he had been in America to satisfy himself as to the security which would be given to the Rosetti Collection when it arrived there.

Here at last was an explanation for his silence. Happy to think that her judgment of him had been wrong, and that he had not forgotten his offer to show her his jewellery, she immediately penned him a note of acceptance and was addressing the envelope when her employer walked in.

Nothing escaped her sharp black eyes and she immediately saw the card. 'From the Conte Rosetti, eh?'

Erica couldn't stop herself from flushing. 'How can you recognize his writing upside down?'

'I didn't – I recognized the crest!'

'He has invited me to see his collection,' Erica explained, forestalling the next, most obvious question.

'Of course you will accept! It is a wonderful opportunity.' The Signora smiled. 'The Conte has an interest in a pretty face.'

'Then that's a guarantee for my safety!'

'What a thing to say! You are a lovely girl.'

'It's my new dress that's lovely,' Erica replied. 'I bought it on Saturday.'

'It suits you. I am glad you are taking an interest in your appearance. What will you wear for your dinner?'

'It's lunch.' Erica looked mischievous. 'Sorry to spoil your romantic illusion!'

'What is wrong with the afternoon?' the Signora retorted, and laughed throatily as she saw Erica blush. 'Seriously, child, beware of him. He is very much a man of the world and I do not wish to see you hurt.'

'I'm only being invited to see the collection,' Erica reiterated, anxious not to let her employer's imagination affect her own.

'A man in the Conte's position does not usually invite shop assistants to lunch with him in his *palazzo*.'

'He could hardly bring the collection round to the local coffee shop!'

'You know what I mean, Erica. I feel responsible for you and—'

'The days of the bold black knights are over, *signora*. Damsels don't remain in distress for long. They all know how to do the karate chop!'

'Do *you*?'

'Actually I don't; but I've a marvellous high kick!'

The Signora chuckled and turned her attention to business. The necklace Erica had been working on was finished, and had been sent to Signor Bruno who had immediately bought it for his wife. His delight had prompted Erica to design several more pieces, and from these Signora Botelli chose a couple of rings and three brooches.

'Make the sapphire and diamond ring first. The others you may do in any order you wish.'

'I'll need a large sapphire,' Erica warned.

'I'll bring you a selection from Rome.' The woman picked up the design in question. 'A bracelet and necklace to match this ring would be ideal. We could get a good price for a whole suite.'

'Let me do the ring first.'

'Would you like someone to help you?'

Erica shook her head and the Signora let the matter drop.

But in the ensuing days she went out of her way to keep her young assistant tied to the work bench, even though this meant she herself had to spend more time in the shop.

By Friday night Erica was beginning to wish she had never submitted the designs, for her eyes ached as much as her fingers, and she vowed that come what may, on Saturday she was going to serve in the shop and not look at a soldering iron, let alone touch it.

Luckily there was an influx of American tourists, and both she and her employer were kept busy serving, too busy even for Erica to give much thought to her visit to the Palazzo Rosetti the next day. It was only as she opened the safe to take out a pair of earrings to show a honeymooning American couple, and caught sign of an aquamarine pendant which Claudia Medina had brought in to have repaired, that she realized she would be seeing the Conte in a matter of hours. Had the pendant been one of *his* gifts to the beautiful widow, or had it come from another admirer? Quickly she pushed the thought away.

At closing time Signora Botelli asked Erica if she would like to borrow some jewellery for the following day. But Erica declined, explaining that she would feel uncomfortable wearing something that did not belong to her.

'Have you decided on your dress?' Signora Botelli asked.

'It depends if it's warm.'

'No cardigan,' the Italian woman asserted. 'Always the English wear the cardigan.'

Erica chuckled. 'A twin set and pearls, you mean! No, I won't wear that. But please don't talk about it any more, or you'll make me so nervous that I won't go.'

'How could you refuse?' came the shocked response.

'By telephoning and saying I have a headache.'

'The Conte would know it was an excuse.'

'Then that should make him all the keener,' Erica retorted, hiding a smile.

'I do not think so. He is not used to chasing women. It is more the other way around.'

'Well, if he doesn't do any chasing, perhaps you'll start to believe that his invitation is purely a business one.'

'Business, possibly,' said the Signora, 'pure, never!'

'You're incorrigible,' Erica scolded, and bidding her employer good night, went home.

It was well after eight o'clock and she accepted the fact that from now until the end of the tourist season they would rarely close before this hour. Late afternoon and evening was their busiest time, for most tourists gave the morning and afternoon over to sightseeing or leisurely tours, only getting down to the serious business of buying when the galleries and museums were shut.

Evening in Venice was the best time as far as Erica was concerned, and definitely the most beautiful time in which to see San Marco Square. The façade of the cathedral gleamed pale and beautiful in the radiance of floodlighting, while the glittering shops that ranged the three other sides of the square glowed like Aladdin's cave from behind the graceful columns that went to form the arcade beneath which one walked. Resisting the urge to stop and treat herself to a coffee, she returned to her apartment where she made herself a light supper, too tired to do more than eat it quickly and then relax in a chair beside the narrow balcony.

Tomorrow she would be seeing Filippo Rosetti. It was a nerve-racking thought and she tried not to let it worry her. She would only be with him for a couple of hours. Nothing momentous could happen to her in that short space of time.

CHAPTER FOUR

ERICA's first waking thought was that in a matter of hours she would be lunching in a palace. Her second was the rueful one that had she not been reluctant to feed Signora Botelli's imagination, she would have asked that good lady for more information about the Rosetti family and their home.

All she had managed to glean was that the Conte lived there with his sister and niece – his sister having been widowed two years previously – and that he had been the sole heir to the Rosetti fortune, though there were a couple of uncles, aunts and many cousins all anxiously waiting to see if he would marry and produce a son. It seemed surprising that, for this reason alone, the Conte was still single. He must love his freedom if he was not willing to give it up in order to ensure that his name and possessions remained within his own branch of the family. Most Italian men were married long before they reached his age, which she guessed to be in the middle thirties.

Unwilling to continue thinking of the Conte, she washed and set her hair, and by the time she had showered and changed it was time to leave for the *palazzo*.

It stood on the Grand Canal; a vast mansion which she had passed many times on the water-bus without knowing to whom it belonged. Unlike many similar Venetian buildings, this one was in excellent repair, and even though the outer walls of the ground floor were green from the dampness of the canal water which lapped its sides, it was a discoloration that came from natural causes and not from lack of money. The rest of the *palazzo* was in splendid, almost ostentatiously excellent condition, with gilded decoration round the innumerable narrow, arched windows and black-lead paint resplendent on the ornately carved balconies and railings.

Ignoring the temptation to take a private gondola, Erica

queued for the water-bus, feeling rather solitary among the crowd of vociferous Italian families, the men plump and suave in pale suits and paler ties, the women matronly in black. With her shining pale gold hair and simple shantung dress and jacket, Erica looked ludicrously different, though it was a difference that the men appreciated, if the scowling looks of their womenfolk were anything to go by.

She had no difficulty obtaining a seat in the bus, for several gallants offered her their own, and though she would have preferred to stand and enjoy the breeze on deck, sitting down at least saved her from the ignominy of having her bottom pinched, an act which seemed – as far as she was aware – to be a national disease that gripped most Italian males between the age of seventeen and seventy.

Long before they reached the *palazzo* she saw it gleaming ahead of her, the gaily painted wooden stakes to which visiting gondolas were tied standing like bright sentinels in the dark green water. The bus stopped some twenty yards away from it, and she walked slowly along the side of the Grand Canal, only realizing – as she drew nearer – that the main entrance lay down a side turning.

The *palazzo* was so vast that it occupied one complete section of the block and though the front of it gave on to the water, its east and west sides were bordered by trees and a flower-filled garden. It was a garden that Erica missed most since living in Venice, and she would have loved to linger on the small but lush lawns that lay either side of the grey stone path that led up to the two shallow steps and the massive wooden door which, a few seconds after her ring, swung back as though on well-oiled casters.

A servant, resplendent in dark blue and silver livery, ushered her in to what, at first glimpse, appeared to be a slightly smaller version of Westminster Abbey but which, as her eyes grew accustomed to the dimness, she saw to be a hall of vast but noble proportions. Its stone walls were lined with magnificent tapestries and a range of windows faced the Grand Canal, with another vast door lying between them. It was shut and bolted, though she assumed it was used when large receptions were held here. What a magnificent sight it must be when all the wooden stakes had gondolas moored against their sides and brilliantly garbed men and women entered the hall the way they had done for hundreds of years past.

Aware of the footman waiting for her – he could not be designated as anything less – she followed him up the stone staircase to the first floor. Here was another hall, half the size of the one below, yet still enormous – one shuddered to think of the heating bills – with massive wooden doors leading off both sides of it. The footman opened the second one and Erica entered a high-ceilinged room filled with people. Her first feeling was of intense and illogical disappointment that she was not to be the only guest. Then quickly her mind took control of her emotions and she knew that she should be pleased that the Conte would not be able to focus his full attention on her. Yet oddly enough she had been looking forward to sparring with him; showing him that though she looked what he had called a gentle creature, she was also an intelligent one.

He came towards her, more handsome than she had remembered in a light grey suit that made his skin look olive. The people around her were equally well dressed, and she wondered if Italians were ever casual when they entertained. More than any other race they loved the opportunity of showing off.

'I am delighted you were able to come.' The Conte lightly touched her hand with his own and led her further into the room, introducing her to several of the guests.

She did not attempt to remember their names beyond being aware that most of them had titles of one sort or another and seemed to come from varying parts of Europe. There were barons and baronesses, *condes* and *condesas,* lords and ladies. Only as he reached his sister did her host stop his introductions.

'I think I will leave Miss Rayburn with you, Anna,' he said, and turned to look directly at the girl beside him. 'Forgive me for leaving you, *signorina,* but as you see, I am not alone.'

'I'm sure I'll be well taken care of,' she smiled, and was both glad and disappointed when he moved away.

'This was going to be a quiet Sunday lunch,' Mrs. Charters said, and Erica forced herself to pay attention. Today the woman looked less tired, though she still gave the impression of being under a strain.

'You aren't telling me all these people just dropped in?' Erica smiled as she accepted a glass of champagne from a magnificent silver tray held out by another liveried servant.

'Not quite that,' the older woman replied. 'Apart from the family and yourself there were only going to be two other guests. Then a couple telephoned to say they would be in Venice for the week-end and some more friends of Filippo's arrived unexpectedly in their yacht.'

'So, like Topsy, the party just growed,' Erica responded.

'A tendency that my brother's parties generally have!' Mrs. Charters' sad eyes were filled with humour, making her look both prettier and younger. 'Filippo is renowned for his entertaining.'

Among other things, Erica added to herself, and looked around as she sipped the delicious champagne. No non-vintage plonk for the fabulously wealthy Conte. This was French and bore a name as famous as his own.

It was two o'clock before they sat down to lunch and well after three before they rose from it. As Mrs. Charters had said, the Conte offered a wonderful table, and for the first time in her life Erica tasted caviar, mounds of it being served with a total disregard to its exorbitant cost. This was followed by consommé and then by individual baby chickens served on an aromatic bed of rosemary, the whole garnished with a succulent assortment of fresh spring vegetables. Large thick spears of Italian asparagus brought the meal to a close, and coffee and liqueurs were served in the drawing-room.

Only when the last of the cups had been cleared away did

two men in dark suits appear. Erica knew at once that they were detectives, and sure enough their arrival heralded the showing of the Rosetti Collection. It was wheeled in on four long wooden trolleys, each one covered with hand-tooled leather boxes. The guests crowded around, but as if by common consent – though it might have been the warning looks given to them by the two plain-clothes men – they remained some two feet away, as the Conte himself moved along each trolley and lifted the lids.

Erica had never seen such a breathtaking display. The best in Florentine craftsmanship was disclosed to her, and gold work of an intricacy she had never imagined was visible not in one but in a hundred different pieces. And not just magnificent craftsmanship but magnificent jewels too: emeralds, diamonds, rubies and sapphires brought the colours of the rainbow into the room. Here was not merely a king's ransom but a kingdom's ransom. She longed for a closer more leisurely inspection of some of the articles, and watched with regret as the boxes were closed and the trolley wheeled away.

This was the signal for the luncheon party to break up, and in twos and threes the guests departed. Erica saw it as her own signal to leave, but moving over to make her farewells to the Conte, found him shaking his head at her.

'Go and talk to my sister,' he said softly. 'I do not wish you to leave yet.'

'But everyone else is going.'

'All the more reason for you to stay.'

'But—'

'You wanted to see my collection.'

'I have.'

He shook his head but was prevented from explaining by several more of his guests coming to say good-bye. Erica returned to sit next to his sister, who was looking extremely pale.

'Aren't you feeling well, Mrs. Charters?'

'I'm tired. I've been ill, you know, and I still tire easily. I'll go and lie down as soon as everyone has gone.'

'That might not be for another half hour.'

'Oh no, Filippo hates protracted good-byes. Sometimes I tell him he makes people leave too abruptly, but he won't listen to me. He says that when someone decides to go, they should go quickly.'

'I agree with him.'

'Most people do,' his sister smiled. 'The thing about Filippo is that he is so frequently right!'

Erica remained silent, unwilling to enter into a discussion of the Conte's habits. She had not seen his niece and to change the subject she asked Mrs. Charters where her daughter was.

'She had an argument with her uncle this morning and is staying in her room. You know about the brooch, of course, so you can imagine how furious he still is with her. She just has to do the slightest thing wrong and he jumps on her.'

'Have you lived with your brother for long?'

'Since my husband was killed.'

'Killed? I'm sorry, I didn't know.'

'He was shot. We were living in Bolivia at the time – my husband was a diplomat – and there was a skirmish at the Embassy.'

'How awful for you!' The words were totally inadequate, but the woman seemed gratified by them.

'I'm just beginning to recover from the shock. My brother has been wonderful: so kind and understanding. Men normally don't have patience with a woman who suffers from nerves.'

Erica found it difficult to believe that the Conte could ever be kind and understanding – let alone in such a situation. She would have thought a nervous woman would be the quickest thing to arouse his temper.

The room had now emptied and with only the three of them there, it seemed enormous. There were at least a dozen settees in varying shades of gold and green brocade, with twice as many armchairs and a preponderance of the small gilt and marble tables beloved by Italians. The furniture did not have the flashiness usually found in the antique shops of Venice and Rome. The carving had been done by hand: the gold leaf was genuine and not gilt, and the ormolu that decorated the heavier pieces bore the dulled patina of age. The walls were lined with damask and hung with recognizable Old Masters. A Bellini, a magnificent Titian, a group of priceless Bernini drawings, their lines still clear and pure despite their great age, and a splendid Canaletto above the marble fireplace.

'You like the paintings?' the Conte said, and she realized he had been watching her for the last few minutes.

'Very much,' she replied, and wished her voice did not sound so nervous. Just because she was sitting in one of Venice's most resplendent palaces, being stared at with interest by one of its wealthiest sons, was no reason to buckle at the knees. What had happened to her true British socialism?

'Will you forgive me, Filippo, if I go to my room and rest?' the Conte's sister asked him.

'Of course,' he replied, and escorted her to the door. He remained there until she disappeared down the hall, then he closed it and came back to stand by the fireplace. It was a warm day, but the logs in it were blazing.

'I suppose it's always chilly in a *palazzo*,' Erica murmured.

'We have excellent central heating!'

'That doesn't overcome the damp, though.'

'That is one of the penances of living in Venice. I always say that in my next incarnation I will return as a duck!'

'A swan,' she corrected, and went scarlet as he smiled widely.

'Thank you for the compliment, Miss Rayburn, though I do believe that ducks are better-natured. Swans have a tendency to bite the hand that feeds them.'

'*You* would give them a very aristocratic bite!'

He laughed outright. '*You* at least know that my bark is much worse!'

It was her turn to laugh and he nodded, as though pleased by the sound, and came to sit beside her. She was aware of his nearness and noticed again how impeccably dressed he was.

'It was kind of you to invite me here to lunch.' She broke the silence, finding its continuation oppressive.

'I promised you that I would.'

'I know you did. But when I didn't – I mean when you – er . . . I'm surprised you remembered,' she finished flatly.

'I cannot imagine any man forgetting a promise he made to *you*.'

'Please don't flirt with me, Conte Rosetti.' She jumped to her feet, unaware that she had done so until she saw him below her. He was still sitting down, his dark head leaning against the back of the settee, one leg crossed nonchalantly over the other.

'I am not flirting with you, Miss Rayburn, I am stating a fact. You are a charming young woman: cool and clear as water.'

'Cold and transparent?' she added.

'Deceptively calm and penetrating everywhere without a sound!'

'I suppose that's some sort of a compliment,' she said doubtfully.

'You have asked me not to give you any,' he reminded her. 'And again let me hasten to add that I was merely stating a fact.' With a suddenness that took her by surprise he jumped up, showing that despite his air of ease he was as tightly coiled as a spring. 'I promised that I would show you my collection. Come with me.'

'But I've already seen it.'

'From a distance and surrounded by people? Credit me with more understanding than that.'

Not waiting to see if she were following him, he went down the hall to a door at the far end. This led to a small ante-room and thence to a library with massive mahogany furniture, leather armchairs and book-lined walls.

In the centre of the room stood the trolleys, still guarded by the two men she had seen earlier. The Conte signalled them to go, and as they did, he lifted the lids of the calf-bound boxes and beckoned Erica forward.

Nervously she stepped closer, and then forgot her nervousness as she feasted her eyes once more on this most priceless collection.

'You may pick up anything you like,' he said.

She shook her head, but within a moment succumbed to the temptation and lifted out one piece after the other. As she came to the Rosetti Rose she paused, but a strange reluctance to touch it made her turn instead to the emerald brooch that lay beside it. It was a perfect stone, flawless and of a deep, clear green.

'Do you like it?' the Conte asked.

'I love emeralds.'

'It isn't your stone. You should wear pearls; pink ones for preference. Emeralds and diamonds are too hard for you.'

'You have very definite likes and dislikes.' She stared down at the brooch.

'I know the sort of things that *you* should wear.' He came close to her. 'For example, I admire your clothes. They are inexpensive, but they show excellent taste.'

He was so serious that she could not be annoyed with him. Nevertheless she did not feel inclined to let his words go unremarked. 'Most women would object to that sort of comment.'

'I would not make such a comment to "most women".'

Once again he had had the last word and she concentrated on the brooch she was holding. 'This hasp is broken. When was the last time you had every piece examined?'

'Not for many years. Most of the jewellery is never worn, and as long as it remains in the vaults it is pointless to do any repairs to it.'

'What a pity that it's all locked away. I feel jewels only come alive when they're being worn.'

'I agree with you. But they need to be worn by a beautiful

49

woman for them to look their best!'

He took the emerald brooch from her, and as his fingers touched hers it was as though an electric current went through her. It was not surprising really, for he had a magnetic quality that had nothing to do with his wealth or position. Undoubtedly his name and rank added to his aura, but even without such trappings he was not a man one could overlook.

'I refuse to believe that you don't know any women beautiful enough to wear these things,' she said, turning away to look at the leather cases.

'I know many beautiful women,' he replied, 'and all of them eager to wear this collection. But my ancestors made it a rule that only Rosetti women could do so, and at the moment there are only two who qualify; my sister and my niece.'

'Then you have an excellent motive for getting married.'

'When I do, it will not be to provide a background to the jewels but a jewel to the background!'

She smiled and he smiled back, looking younger and less aloof. 'Nevertheless you have a point about my keeping the jewellery in good repair,' he continued. 'When it comes back from America I will arrange for you to examine each piece and decide what needs to be done.'

'That would involve a lot of work.' At random she picked up a necklace: a ribbon of ruby fire. 'Just examining the collection will take a week, and doing the repairs could be a six months' job. I might not be here that long.'

'You are thinking of leaving Venice?' he asked sharply. 'Do you not like it here?'

'I love it.'

'Then why do you talk of leaving?'

'Because Italy isn't my home. I can't stay here for ever.' Made nervous by the intensity of his gaze, she put down the ruby necklace and backed away from him. 'It's getting late, Cónte, I must go.'

'We will have tea first and then I will take you home.'

'That isn't necessary.'

'What isn't? The tea or my taking you home?'

'Both. I'm sure you don't normally have tea – and it isn't necessary for you to take me home. I can quite easily go on the bus.'

'Do you not wish me to accompany you?'

'Of course I do, but . . .'

'Then why do you make such a fuss?'

She drew a deep breath. 'I'm not making a fuss. I just don't want to be a bother to you.'

'You are only a bother when you keep arguing. We will have tea and then I will escort you home.'

Back in the salon he rang for a servant while Erica wandered round the room, admiring the many beautiful and priceless objects in it. Half a dozen Fabergé boxes were arranged on the glass shelves of a tall cabinet, while in another one reposed a similar number of jewelled Fabergé eggs, some closed and some open to show the unusual interiors.

'It must be a great responsibility to take care of all this,' she remarked.

'It is. I often think I'd be far happier if I were a self-made man. If you make your own wealth, you have the choice of deciding how to spend it. But if one inherits so much . . .' His black head tilted as his eyes ranged the room. 'Sometimes I feel it to be a ball and chain.'

'What stops you from selling everything?'

'And deny my heritage? Such a thing would be impossible. Besides, most of the time I enjoy it. It is only occasionally that I feel I would prefer to be poor and unknown. At least if I were, I would never have any doubts about the sincerity of my friends.'

Without being told, she knew he was really referring to women. Sympathy for him warmed her, melting some of her reserve. To think of the Conte as a man looking for genuine friendship made him less frightening than to see him as the head of one of Italy's leading families.

The door opened and two servants came in carrying a

small table which they set in front of the settee nearest to the fireplace. On it was a silver tea-set and a beautifully worked Florentine coffee pot in gold.

'The coffee is for you?' she surmised.

There was an unmistakable twinkle in his eyes. 'When I said we would have tea together, I meant the participation of the ceremony, not the liquid!'

She laughed and poured him a cup of coffee, trying to keep her hand steady. It was no easy task, for he watched her every movement and, even when she had given him his cup, he continued to watch her as she served herself. The tea was surprisingly strong and milk as well as lemon was provided. Gratefully she added milk and sipped.

'Delicious,' she said. 'It's real English tea.'

'I have it sent from London. My sister prefers it to coffee. It is a legacy left from her marriage.'

'I understand Mr. Charters was killed?'

'Yes. It was a most tragic business. My sister is only now beginning to recover from it. That is why it is so important for her to have no worries.'

Erica found it hard to imagine what worries a member of the Rosetti family could have. Not monetary ones in any event; and other worries could frequently be cushioned by wealth.

'Money doesn't solve one's problems,' he said as though aware of what was going through her mind. 'Frequently it creates them. In Sophie's case, for example. She has—' He stopped as the door opened and a petite, dark-haired woman came in.

With a sense of shock Erica recognized Claudia Medina. The woman was holding out her hands to the man, her face tilted to receive the kiss which he placed on her cheek.

'Filippo, forgive me,' she said in a husky voice. 'I know we weren't supposed to meet till later, but Uncle Otto caught the earlier plane to Paris and it left me free.'

'I thought he was staying until this evening?'

'We finished our discussion during lunch and he was

52

afraid we'd start to quarrel again if he remained any longer! He is even worse than usual. Anyone would think he is still my guardian!'

'He brought you up,' the Conte reminded her.

'But I have been married and widowed since then.' Claudia tossed her head. 'It is foolish of him to treat me as if I were still a single girl. He as good as told me that if I'm not remarried within a year, he'll cut my allowance.'

'I am sure you will find a way of getting around him.'

She shrugged and looked at Erica. 'We have met before somewhere,' she smiled, 'but I cannot quite place it.'

'I work for Signora Botelli,' Erica said.

Instantly the smile thinned and Erica could almost hear the woman's mind working. What was a jewellery assistant doing at the *palazzo*? More important still, why was she taking tea with its owner?

Unwilling to be in the way, Erica stood up. 'Thank you for a delightful afternoon, Conte.' She spoke directly to him, but avoided looking into his face.

'There is no need for you to go yet,' he replied.

Ignoring the comment, she smiled good-bye at Claudia Medina, who stood in front of him, noticing in the split second she focused on them what a handsome couple they made: both dark and olive-skinned; both with black flashing eyes. But where the man was wide-shouldered and full of animal strength, the woman was feminine and fragile.

Swiftly Erica left the room, not even giving the Conte a chance to reach the door and open it for her. Across the long hall she sped and down the flight of stone steps that led to the vast lower hall. Late afternoon sunlight streamed through the windows overlooking the Grand Canal and sent golden shafts across the grey stone floor. The heavy wooden front door was locked and her fingers fumbled at the massive iron bolts. Slowly they slid back, but as she went to open the door itself a long-fingered hand came out to cover her own.

'Why such a precipitate flight?' Filippo Rosetti asked.

Startled, she looked into his face. He was smiling slightly, but she knew he was angry. 'It is late, Conte, and I must be getting back.'

'A little while ago we agreed that *I* would take you home.'

'That was before Signora Medina arrived.'

'What has Claudia's arrival got to do with it?'

'You can't leave her now.'

'I did not ask her to come so early.'

Dumbfounded, she stared at him.

'There is no need to look so concerned,' he continued. 'The fact that Claudia decided to call here much earlier than arranged does not alter the plans I made with you.'

'You made *no* plans with me.'

'Indeed I did.' He held open the door and inclined his head for her to go ahead of him.

'Please don't bother seeing me home,' she protested. 'I'm perfectly capable of going on my own.'

'So you said before. Be careful, Miss Rayburn, or you could become that most obnoxious of all women – an argumentative one! Now please give in gracefully.'

'I've no intention of giving in. Do go back to Signora Medina.'

'I am not a parcel to be sent where you wish,' he retorted.

The simile was so unexpected that she giggled. How ridiculous they must look, standing here quarrelling like a couple of children.

'What have I said that amuses you?' he inquired stiffly.

'Nothing – everything.'

'Make up your mind.'

'You're trying not to let me have one!'

He caught his breath, then expelled it slowly. 'I am used to giving orders,' he said, and as if to prove it, put his hand under her elbow and guided her through the gardens.

They were more extensive than she had realized and appeared even larger because of their beautiful landscaping. In actual area the ground they covered was small, but numerous sections were divided into secluded bowers, each with its own distinctive decor both as to plants and shrubs and statuary. One held a small fountain which spouted a silver mist of water over idly swimming goldfish; another was a mosaiced area filled with flowering urns and a rustic bench; a third was an arbour of white trellis with trailing plants overhead and grass underfoot.

They came to a door set in the wall and the Conte opened it and stepped out on to a small quay. Here were moored two gondolas and a sleek motorboat, on its prow a small flag bearing what she took to be his coat of arms. He helped her into the boat, untied the rope that held it moored and switched on the engine.

Gently they glided along a dark green waterway with tall houses looming either side of them. Erica watched him manipulate the craft. He did it with practised ease, steering it skilfully round corners that seemed too tight for them to turn. At no time did he let out the full throttle but seemed content to move at a leisurely pace through the water. Though she had lived here for six months she was seeing a part of Venice she did not recognize, and only as they emerged from a narrow canal did she discover they were by the harbour. As it was Sunday there was little activity, and large ships, some gleaming white, some dark and rusty, lay on the water like sleeping albatrosses.

'You've brought me the longest way round,' she accused.

'I thought it would give us a chance to cool off. When I quarrel with a woman I prefer it to be over something important.'

Uncertain how to answer this, she pretended to be absorbed in the scenery. No matter from what viewpoint one saw the city it was always beautiful, its uniqueness adding to its charm. Nowhere else was squalor and dirt so magnificently intermingled, nowhere else could one find ruins crumbling so gracefully.

'Occasionally I toy with the idea of living elsewhere,' the Conte said behind her, 'but no matter where I go, I am always glad to come back here.'

'I can understand that.'

'Yet you say you are going to leave?'

'That doesn't mean I *want* to go. Merely that all things come to an end. To be young and foreign in a country is difficult enough, but to be old and foreign is impossible.'

He flung her a look of astonishment. 'What is this talk of being old? You are still a child.'

'Children grow up,' she smiled. 'Anyway, I only came here to break out of the rut. I couldn't make it my permanent home.'

'Could you do so if you had a family here?'

She shrugged and turned back to look at the water gliding past them. Her entire body was quivering as if all her nerve ends were exposed. She knew it came from the strong impact this man was making on her and she tried to analyse it away. She was not unused to male companionship or admiration. Living in a university town where her home had been the focal point for many students, she had become accustomed to compliments. Yet here she was acting like an ingénue to the ones Conte Rosetti was making. But complimentary was not the right way to describe his manner of talking to her. He was too subtle; and it was this which disarmed her, making her see how vulnerable she was. The Conte was a man of the world, used to women of the world, a description which she knew she could never fulfil. A picture of Claudia Medina came into her mind and she wondered if the woman was truly his mistress or whether only gossip made her so. Yet according to Signora Botelli the Conte paid her jewellery bills, a gesture he would scarcely do for someone who was merely a friend. What a dangerous and disarming lover he would make, demanding total obedience yet – because he was too intelligent to be satisfied with a compliant female – wanting the woman to have a mind of her own. The thought was disturbing and she tried to depersonalize it, forcing herself to think only of man and woman, rather than of this particular couple.

Because of her upbringing Erica had never been able to envisage herself as someone's mistress. It seemed to be a degrading position that demanded more from the woman than the man. Yet most of the girls she knew did not agree with her. They believed that a woman's love-life could be as unrestricted as that of a man's. They saw no stigma in an unmarried sexual relationship, and the fact that she herself still did was a mark of her immaturity. Would she feel the same sense of repugnance about it if she fell significantly in love? She had been attracted to several men in the past three years, but for none of them had she experienced the feeling which would have made her consider the world well lost for love. If she ever did, then perhaps she too might behave like many of her girl friends.

'Come back to Venice, Miss Rayburn. Your thoughts are miles away!'

The Conte's voice broke into her reverie and she turned swiftly and apologized. They had reached a more familiar part of the city and were approaching a bridge which, if she crossed it, would bring her into the street where she lived.

He lessened speed and drew the motorboat into the side. With a lithe movement he jumped out and bent to help her. The step was slippery and he caught her round the waist and lifted her bodily from the launch. His hands were like steel around her and she knew it had required enormous strength to have lifted her up from such a position. Yet he gave no sign of exertion and looked as relaxed as ever as he jumped back into the cockpit.

'*Arrivederci*,' he called, and turning the engine full throttle, roared away.

His quick departure left her unaccountably let down. But what else had she expected him to do? Stand there and mutter inanities? He had already given her far more of his time than she had anticipated. Besides, Claudia Medina was awaiting his return.

The knowledge was depressing and briskly she crossed the bridge and turned towards her apartment. She had spent a wonderful afternoon with interesting people in magnificent surroundings, and had concluded the expedition by being escorted almost to her front door by the city's most handsome, aristocratic member. What more could a twenty-three-year-old English girl with an ordinary background and no pretensions expect?

CHAPTER FIVE

As Erica had anticipated, she was required to give Signora Botelli a complete account of the afternoon she had spent at the Palazzo Rosetti. This included not only a description of the guests, but also the food and furnishings down to the last minute detail.

'It is said to be the best preserved *palazzo* in Venice,' the woman informed her.

'It's certainly the most opulent. There's a Titian in the salon which is worthy of a museum, and some Bernini drawings that must be absolutely priceless.'

'They are the only ones in private hands,' the Signora said.

'What does the Conte do?' Erica asked casually, as she dusted one of the glass-topped counters. 'I know he doesn't need to work, but I can't see him being idle.'

'He is never idle. He has an insurance company and a bank.'

Erica made a face. 'I'm not sure I approve of so much power. It's wrong for one family to have so much.'

'There is also the Rosetti Foundation. They give millions away to all kinds of charities.'

'Conscience money!' Erica retorted.

'I don't think the Conte has any guilt about his money. If he helps others, he does it from a sense of duty. Anyway,' the Signora smiled, 'you mustn't be derogatory about one of our clients.'

'He's never bought a thing here!'

'Signora Medina has! Which reminds me – she's coming in this morning. Is her pendant repaired?'

'I finished it on Friday.'

Erica was giving the pendant a final polish when the young widow came in. Although it was early morning she was elegantly dressed, her beige silk suit matching her beige crocodile bag and shoes.

'Of course I remember you now.' She greeted Erica with a smile. 'What a pity I didn't know you were coming to the Palazzo yesterday, or you could have brought the pendant with you.' She took it from Erica and put it on. 'I understand you saw Filippo's collection,' she went on. 'Did you like it?'

'It was magnificent. One doesn't often get the chance to look at such pieces so closely.'

'Filippo thought you would appreciate that best of all. That's why he invited you. He didn't know how else to repay you for the trouble Sophie caused.'

'Miss Charters caused no trouble,' Erica said quickly, surprised that Claudia Medina should know about it. Yet why shouldn't the Conte confide in her? After all, she was a close friend of the family as well as his.

Signora Botelli came out of the office and greeted her customer with friendly deference. 'We will be producing some new designs in about a month. If you are interested in anything particularly . . .'

'A bracelet and earrings to match my pendant.' Claudia Medina looked at herself in the full-length mirror that took up most of the end wall. She lifted her thick, glossy black hair to disclose two shell-like lobes. 'Something dangling, I think.'

'You will need to wear your hair drawn back,' the Signora advised.

'Of course. The Conte likes it that way.' Through the mirror Claudia Medina smiled at the woman. 'He is a man of definite tastes.'

'He knows his mind,' the Signora agreed.

Claudia Medina delicately lowered her eyes, though watching her, Erica felt that the modesty was false, assumed only to create the image she wished to project. For all her air of fragility, Claudia Medina had a will of iron. If she gave in to a man it was because it paid her to do so. Watching as she tried on several more pieces and postured in front of the mirror, Erica marvelled that any man – particularly one like the Conte – could be taken in by such false gentleness. Surely he was intelligent enough to see the wilfulness in the full mouth, the hardness in the large eyes? But perhaps he did not care to see beyond the façade.

Excusing herself from the shop, Erica went to work at the jewellers' bench. But long after the lovely widow had left, her perfume lingered behind, souring the rest of the day. The jealousy Erica felt for the woman both astonished and frightened her, the more so because she knew it stemmed from the strange emotions which the Conte Rosetti was arousing in her.

Anxious to disprove them, she went out to dinner with Johnny Rogers, a young man from the American Express office who had been pursuing her for months.

He was delighted at her change of heart and set out to be as entertaining as possible. To begin with she found it hard to stop being self-conscious. She had the strange feeling that Filippo Rosetti was hiding behind every corner and that whenever she looked up she would find his dark eyes watching her. The notion was ludicrous, born out of her inability to forget him, and it was not until she had drunk half a bottle of Chianti that the image of him began to dull and she was able to look into her escort's blunt features without seeing narrow patrician ones.

'We must do this more often,' Johnny said as he took her home. 'How are you fixed for the week-end?'

She longed to say she was busy, but resolutely told him she was free, and before bidding him good night, agreed to see him on Saturday evening.

Alone again in her apartment she felt such a blessed relief that she could understand why she had been foolish enough to have gone out with Johnny in the first place, nor why she had promised to go out with him again. He was charming and intelligent, yet all the while she had kept comparing him with Filippo Rosetti. The knowledge filled her with dread. She hardly knew the Italian yet she could not stop thinking about him. How much of this stemmed from the awe with which Signora Botelli referred to him, she did not know; all she did know was that the man had mesmerized her.

Slowly the week passed. Johnny telephoned her twice at the shop and would have done so more frequently had she not told him, after his second call, that he was incurring Signora Botelli's wrath.

'Far be it for me to upset the dear old pouter pigeon,' he chuckled, and promised not to call again until Saturday.

His description of the Signora was so apt that she was smiling as she put down the receiver, and felt very guilty when her employer – seeing the smile on her face – said happily:

'I am so pleased you have found yourself a boy-friend. I do not think that having lunch with the Conte Rosetti did you much good. You have been pale and sad ever since.'

'Green with envy, perhaps,' Erica said quickly.

'You are not the jealous type; at least not over money or possessions.' The plump chin quivered. 'Over a man you might be different. But even then you are the type who would suffer in silence rather than fight for what you wanted.'

'My character isn't as milky as my colouring!'

'I do not mean you lack spirit,' the Signora hastened to assure her. 'But you have pride. And that will not allow you to fight for a man.'

'Then I'd better not fall for one with a roving eye!'

'One cannot fall in love to order.' The Signora glanced at the telephone. 'The American boy who calls – he has lost his heart to you?'

'We're just good friends,' Erica said flatly.

'In today's language that means lovers! When Signora Medina calls the Conte her friend, she is—'

The entry of two customers put an end to further conversation, and by the time they were alone again the Signora's mind was working on another tack.

But Erica could not forget what had been said, and later that evening as she sat in her room she tried to assess Claudia Medina's character from all she had gleaned from Signora Botelli. Married at seventeen to a wealthy Milanese industrialist, the woman had been widowed three years ago. Her family was a well-known Roman one with more pride than money, and though she did not appear to be short of money herself, it was rumoured that she had not been left as well off as she pretended.

'The Conte would solve all her problems,' Signora Botelli had stated, 'both financially and emotionally! He is a real man, that one.'

How much of a man, Erica knew all too well. Her body tingled at the mere thought of him; his presence was like an aura around her, heightening her senses and disturbing her peace of mind.

To combat it, she went out frequently with Johnny during the following week. But no matter how hard she tried, she could not see him as anything more than a friend.

As celebration of their fifth meeting he took her to the Danielli for dinner and went to great pains to make sure they had a table on the terrace. It gave them a panoramic view of Venice, though the diners around them – either American or English – made it hard to believe they were abroad. Had it not been for the menu and the waiters they could have been in any smart restaurant in any cosmopolitan city.

'I wish I'd been born in an era when travelling abroad was still a great adventure,' she commented.

'What a thing to say to me,' Johnny grinned. 'Don't you know I'm the king of the package tour? A couple of years from now and I'll have my own agency.'

'Do you want that sort of responsibility?'

'Sure. You can't make big money working for someone else.'

'And you consider big money important?'

'I like the nice life, honey, and you can't have that without bread. 'His grey eyes appraised her. 'Aren't you ambitious?'

'Not for money. I love designing jewellery, but I don't particularly want to own it.'

63

'Yet you make beautiful things for rich women. Don't you envy their ability to buy anything they want?'

'I never envy anyone their possessions.' She bit her lip. 'I'm making myself sound too good to be true!'

'You are too good,' he grinned. 'How about showing me some of your vices?'

'My only vice is that I'm a prude.'

He raised his brows. 'Is that a vice?'

'Most men seem to think so,' she smiled. 'I doubt if you'll be any different!'

'Ouch!' he said plaintively. 'That remark hurt. But probably because it fits me!'

She laughed at his honesty and liked him all the more for it, though not enough to change her mind when he tried to turn their goodnight kiss into a more lengthy one.

'I'm still going to try and seduce you,' he said, 'so be warned.'

'That's as good as being forearmed,' she replied, and heard him laugh as she closed the door on him.

Sunday was the hottest day she had known since her arrival in Venice, and she regretted her refusal to go with Johnny to the Lido beach. It was too sultry to remain indoors, and at lunchtime she went to a local restaurant and treated herself to ravioli and scampi, then debated whether to go to the Lido for a swim. Knowing the interest her silvery-blonde colouring would arouse, she decided against it, and instead went for a stroll in the Piazza San Marco.

The shops were closed, but the cafés were open, their tables packed with tourists and Venetians all enjoying the Sunday afternoon. Hundreds of pigeons weaved and circled overhead, swooping to the ground to be fed corn seeds and crumbs. Erica felt she must be the only person without anyone to share the day, and experienced such a pang of self-pity that she decided to overcome it by treating herself to an icecream.

After some effort she managed to find a vacant table, shaded from the sun by the arcade yet still giving her a good view of the square. A few yards away came music from another café: Franz Léhar waltzes that epitomized Venice as much as they did the Vienna where they had originated. A glass of water and a vanilla ice were set before her and she picked up a spoon and began to eat. In a pale yellow cotton dress that highlighted her softly tanned skin, she looked as cool as an ice herself. Because of the heat she had held her hair away from her face with a narrow circlet of gold, a gift from Signora Botelli. Unsoftened by her hair, her features were thrown into relief: her eyes large and limpid and marked by delicately arched brows; her nose small and straight and her mouth looking soft and tremulous and the warm pink of a rose.

All around her people were talking to friends and family, and again self-pity threatened to engulf her. She forced herself to concentrate on the beautiful façade of the church. Her eyes moved over the statues that stood in marble and gilded splendour along its length, then came down to the entrance, where a flock of nuns hovered.

A young couple caught her attention, not so much because the girl was young and pretty but because the man looked like one of the Apostles. He was tall and thin, with light brown hair, worn long and straight, and a full beard. Even as she watched he put his arm around the girl's waist and drew her away from the church. It was only then that Erica realized that the girl was the Conte Rosetti's niece. Startled, she stared at the bearded man again. From his colouring she did not think he was Italian, while from his strange appearance – apart from his long hair and beard he wore a long white shirt embroidered with blue and gold motifs – it was highly improbable that he was on the Rosetti visiting list.

She was still watching the couple when the girl turned in the direction of the Grand Canal. As she did so she stopped and glanced apprehensively at the man beside her. Then she caught his hand and began to walk swiftly towards the arcade.

It was only as she came abreast of Erica's table that she stopped, her smile so wide that it was difficult to believe this was the same unfriendly girl she had met at the *palazzo* a fortnight ago.

'Hello, Miss Rayburn, how wonderful to see you!'

Surprised by the warmth of the greeting, Erica was even more so when the girl asked if she could join her and sat down without waiting for confirmation.

'David, go!' she cried. 'Quickly!'

'You're wrong, Sophie.' The man's voice was low and gentle. 'Let me stay.'

'I know what I'm doing. For goodness' sake, go!'

The man melted into the crowd and Sophie gave a sigh of relief and leaned back in her chair, at the same time reaching out for Erica's half-finished icecream.

'I'm not mad,' she said hurriedly as she saw the look on Erica's face. 'I can't explain yet. Just play along with me. *Please.*'

'What do you want me to do?'

'Personally I'd sell all my uncle's paintings for a couple of Jackson Pollocks,' Sophie said brightly. 'We'll just have to agree to differ when it comes to art.'

'Still talking like a Philistine?' a deep voice inquired, and Erica had no need to turn to know who had come to stand beside them. She also knew the reason for Sophie's illogical conversation and behaviour. The girl had obviously seen her uncle in the square and did not wish him to guess she had been with a man. Hence her sudden dash to this table and her pretence that she was in the middle of a conversation with Erica – as well as an icecream!

Annoyed at being made use of in this way, Erica was in half a mind to make her anger known. But the look of pleading in Sophie's brown eyes kept her silent, and she watched wordlessly as the Conte pulled out the vacant chair beside her and sat down.

'I did not know you had a rendezvous with Miss Rayburn,' he said pleasantly to his niece.

'I didn't realize I had to tell you *all* my engagements,' the girl replied.

'Of course you don't. But had I known your plans, I

would have joined you earlier.' He smiled at Erica. 'You are well?'

'Yes, thank you.'

'But somewhat pale. May I get you a drink?'

She shook her head, forbearing to explain that her pallor was due to his niece's behaviour.

Accepting her refusal, he ordered a coffee for himself. It was exactly a fortnight since she had seen him, yet she felt it was only yesterday, so constantly had he been in her mind. It angered her that she should have been so aware of him when he was so apparently unaware of *her*. If he had given her half as much thought, he would have telephoned her or come to the shop days ago. Obliquely she looked at him. As always he was fastidiously dressed, this time in blue-grey, with a slightly paler shirt. A gold watch glinted on his wrist, where the hairs grew thick and black, though the hands themselves were pale and smooth, the fingers supple and strong. Moving her eyes upward, she studied his face. He looked unconcerned as he sipped his coffee, but there was a narrowing of the thin mouth that indicated that he was holding himself under control, and the sharp glint in his eyes suggested the same thing. Was he angry because his niece was spending the afternoon with a shop assistant? She dismissed the thought at once. The Conte might be a snob, but he was not a fool, and having already invited her to his home he could not object if a member of his family wished to renew the acquaintance.

His head turned swiftly and Erica found herself looking directly into black pupils. She lowered her lids, her long lashes resting on cheeks that were pink with embarrassment.

'What were you and Sophie talking about?' he asked softly.

'Art,' Erica replied. 'Your niece likes the moderns.'

'Ah yes, Jackson Pollock. And what about you?'

'My taste is eclectic – in art as well as jewellery.'

'I understand you are designing some modern pieces for Signora Medina?'

Erica's heart missed a beat, but she managed to nod her head. 'She wants a bracelet and earrings to match a pendant she bought from us.'

'It is a lovely pendant,' he said. 'Did *you* make it?'

'I designed it, but it was made in Signora Botelli's own workshop.'

'What about designing something for me?' Sophie came into the conversation saucily.

'Time enough for that when you have a husband to pay your bills,' her uncle chided.

'*You're* not Claudia's husband!'

The Conte caught his breath and for an instant looked furious, but when he spoke his voice was soft. 'You have no need to buy jewellery, Sophie. You may choose to wear anything from my collection.'

'It's too much bother. Anyway, aren't you scared I might be tempted to sell it?'

'You will not make the same mistake twice.' His tone was even more gentle. 'Not because you would worry about *my* anger, but because you know it would break your mother's heart.'

'I hate you for telling her what I did!'

'It was the only way of making sure you didn't repeat the act.' He pointed to the icecream melting in front of her. 'Finish it up, your mother is approaching.'

Sophie jumped up as Anna Charters stopped beside the table.

At once her brother went to pull a chair forward for her, but she shook her head. 'I am afraid I cannot stay, Filippo. I'm meeting the Frascattis at four o'clock and I am already late.'

'It is unwise to hurry in this heat,' the Conte warned. 'It is better for me to telephone and say you have been delayed.'

'There won't be any need if I go now.'

'I'll come with you,' Sophie offered.

Her mother nodded and looked at Erica. 'I'm delighted to see you, Miss Rayburn. I hope we meet again soon.'

'Come on, Mother,' the younger girl said impatiently. 'You said you were late.' She beamed at Erica. 'Thanks for the icecream. I'll be in touch with you!'

Mother and daughter wended their way through the crowded tables and were soon lost from sight. Erica glanced nervously at the man beside her and wished he would do the same.

'Don't you have an appointment?' she blurted out.

'I am in no hurry.' He looked at her glass of water and without asking her, ordered two fresh coffees. He did not speak again until they were placed in front of them, then he leaned forward and looked fully into her face. 'It was kind of you not to give my niece away.'

'Wh-what do you mean?'

'You know very well. I saw Sophie with Mr. Gould several moments before *she* saw *me*.'

'You mean you *knew* she wasn't with me?'

'*Si*. You were sitting here by yourself. I saw you. That is why I was walking in this direction.'

She was too busy thinking about the failure of Sophie's subterfuge to pay attention to the rest of what he had said, and only as she looked at him and saw his intent expression did she do so.

'I was going to join you for afternoon tea,' he continued. 'Which reminds me – the Rosetti family owe you an icecream. Poor Sophie thought it would fool me more if she pretended to eat yours!'

Erica's lips twitched. Though sorry that Sophie had not succeeded in fooling her uncle, she was nonetheless amused by the way he was reacting to it.

'Please don't bother getting me another icecream. It's better for my figure if I don't eat one.'

'Not at all. You are too slender. A few kilos would improve you.'

'And more expensive clothes too, no doubt!'

He looked completely unrepentant. 'I am glad that you take note of what I say. It augurs well for the future.'

Deliberately she refrained from asking him what he

meant, though from the way he continued to watch her she knew he was waiting for her to do so. She sipped her coffee. If he was hoping to embarrass her by flirting with her he would have to do better than this. She might be innocent from his viewpoint, but she was not so devoid of social graces that she would allow herself to be flummoxed by such heavy-handed flattery.

'Why was your niece afraid to let you see her with Mr. Gould?' she asked. 'Don't you like young men with beards?'

'It is his attitude to life – not his clothes – that bothers me.'

'What does he do?'

'Nothing. That is the trouble. He has an engineering degree, but according to Sophie he is more interested in meditation. He has been in India for three years and is on his way back to England. Unhappily he decided to stop off in Venice – which is how they met.'

'I take it you don't approve of their friendship?'

'Would you – if you were me?'

She pondered the question. 'Not if I were *you*,' she said finally.

His nostrils flared. 'Explain that.'

'I have a less rigid upbringing than you, Conte Rosetti. I am able to make allowances for different points of view.'

'Are you suggesting I am narrow-minded?'

'Yes. You are also obstinate and self-opinionated.'

His eyes glittered like points of steel. 'All this is based on one single meeting with me?'

'This is the third time we have met.'

'I do not count that time in the shop. We began on the wrong feet.'

'Wrong foot,' she corrected, glad to find he was not faultless in everything.

'Foot, feet, what is the difference! We are talking now of important things. I am disappointed that you should think me narrow-minded. I consider myself to be exactly the opposite!'

'Naturally.' Her tone was dry. 'That's why you object to your niece's friend!'

'She wishes to marry him,' he said abruptly. 'Can you see them being happy?'

In all fairness she had to concede to some reservations, but was quick to add that she was reluctant to give a firm view without talking to the young man.

'He may be quite different from the way he looks,' she finished. 'Anyway, it's better to go to India and study religion than to wear leather suits and tear up the motorway on a motorbike!'

'Both are extremes of behaviour that I detest.'

'Didn't *you* do anything foolish when you were a boy?'

He rubbed one long finger across his chin. 'I had too many family responsibilities to have the time. There was some talk about my entering the priesthood . . .' He smiled, his eyes crinkling. 'That would have been worse than foolish – it would have been a disaster!'

Annoyance seared through her. 'Do continental men *always* talk about sex?'

'I cannot answer for other men,' he replied. 'For myself, the answer is no.'

'Then why—'

'With you it is different. I feel I can say whatever comes into my mind. It is hard for me to realize that we barely know each other. I seem to have thought of nothing except you since we have met.'

She was stunned into silence, and taking advantage of it, he put his hand on her arm. His fingers were warm on her skin and it required all her will power not to pull her hand away. He's only flirting with me, she reminded herself. Whatever he says to the contrary, he's only playing a game.

'Do not let us waste time talking about Sophie and her young man,' he continued. 'I will deal with him in my own way. I wish to talk about you instead. Will you have dinner with me tonight?'

Happiness flooded through her, but as swiftly as it arose,

so it ebbed away. He was only asking her out because he had seen her this afternoon. Had they not met he might never have contacted her again.

'I can't go out with you,' she said stiffly. 'I am busy.'

'What are you doing? Where are you going?'

Unprepared for the catechism, she could not lie, and her silence gave him his answer. His expression hardened.

'Why are you pretending, Erica?'

It was the first time he had spoken her name and she wondered if he was aware of it.

'Why?' he demanded again. 'I insist that you tell me.'

'Do I have to have a reason?'

'Certainly. You are not an irrational child. If you refuse to dine with me, it is because you do not wish to do so. I have a right to know what I have done to offend you.'

He looked so angry and determined that she stared at him helplessly, wondering how to appease him. Yet why should she even *bother* to appease him? She meant nothing in his life and he meant nothing in hers. It was ridiculous for either of them to pretend. She tilted her head and faced him.

'If you hadn't bumped into me – if Sophie hadn't used me – you wouldn't have asked me out.'

'So that's it! You think I only asked you to dine with me because of my niece?' His fingers tightened so painfully on her arm that she winced. But he appeared not to notice it, so intent was he on what he was saying. 'I have invited you to have dinner with me because I want to be with you. I would like to be with you now if I did not already have another engagement.'

'Please don't let me keep you,' she said coldly.

'What's the matter with you? Why are you angry?'

'I am not angry, Conte Rosetti. I just do not like being picked up and dropped like a bad penny when it suits you.'

'Picked up and dropped?' Dark eyebrows met above his long, thin nose. 'I do not comprehend you.'

'It's very simple.' Throwing discretion to the wind, she

72

became blunt. 'It's two weeks since we met, and if you hadn't seen me by accident this afternoon, it might have been another two weeks – or even a month – before you saw me again. In fact you might never have seen me at all! I've already lived here six months without bumping into you.'

'You have already lived twenty-three years without our meeting one another.'

Not sure what to make of this, she stared at him. But his expression gave her no help. A faint flush darkened the tightly stretched skin across his cheeks and his dark eyes were narrow as though in concentration.

'Continue,' he said. 'I wish you to get it all out of your system.'

'There's nothing more to be said. It isn't necessary for me to dot the i's and cross the t's.'

'No, it isn't,' he sighed. 'But it seems that *I* must do a bit of dotting and crossing.'

Once more he leaned close, and she became aware of unexpected lights in the dark brown irises around his pupils; saw too the exceptionally thick, black lashes.

'Since you had lunch at the Palazzo, I have been in London on business. I only returned to Venice late last night. And it was an unexpected return too, for I had not reckoned to be here until next week. If I had known of my change of plans earlier yesterday, I would have telephoned you at the shop. But by the time I knew I could get back, Botelli's was closed and I did not know how else to contact you.'

'Why should you wish to do so?'

'Because I wanted to see you,' he said in exasperation.

'We still only met by accident this afternoon.'

'I was going to telephone you tomorrow. I would have come in search of you today, except that I did not know where you lived.'

Because she wanted to believe him so much, she was afraid to believe him at all. 'It's silly for us to argue, Conte Rosetti. I can't go out with you tonight.'

'You mean you won't!'

She shrugged and was aware of him pushing back his

chair and standing up. 'In that case there is no more to be said. I wish you good afternoon, Erica.' He hesitated. 'You do not mind me calling you by your name. But I have not been thinking of you as Miss Rayburn.'

'English people don't mind having their Christian names used,' she said carelessly, and knew her indifference had piqued him, for he frowned, gave her a polite bow and walked away.

She watched as he made his way across the square. Even among so many people he was noticeable for his tallness and upright carriage. In the sunshine his hair gleamed black as a raven's wing, and lay thick and close to the nape of his neck, stopping short just above the collar of his shirt. A little girl ran across his path and bumped into him. He swooped down and caught her before she fell, then set her on her feet. Still bent, he spoke to her, and though he was too far away for Erica to hear what he said, she saw the child laugh up at him before running away. A crowd of nuns interrupted her line of vision and when their fluttering black robes had gone, so had the Conte.

How strange it had been to hear him speak her name. Everything about his upbringing indicated attention to tradition and for him to call her Erica meant he saw her more as a friend than an acquaintance. Yet they were too socially apart to be friends and to pretend otherwise would be to fool herself. But what about girl-friend? For him to see her as this seemed far more logical. Indeed men of his type often chose their mistresses from outside their own milieu. In this way they avoided the complications that might ensue if they had an affair with someone in their own circle. Against this argument, however, was his relationship with Claudia Medina.

This thought depressed her so much that tears filled her eyes. She groped in her bag for a handkerchief, and as she took it out was aware of a shadow falling across her table. Her heart thumped wildly and she lowered her head further. But the voice that spoke to her was a strange one, and her excitement died as she looked up.

David Gould stood in front of her. 'Would you mind if I joined you?'

'Be my guest,' she said drily. 'Everyone else has this afternoon!'

He smiled and sat down. Seen at close quarters he was as arresting as he had been from a distance, exuding a tranquillity that came more from his calm blue eyes than his white flowing robes. He was in no way the sort of young man she would have associated with Sophie Charters, any more than she would have seen Sophie appealing to him.

'The Conte has gone?' he asked, giving the title its English pronunciation.

'You wouldn't be sitting here with me otherwise!'

'I have nothing against him,' he shrugged. 'All the bad vibrations are *his*.'

She grinned, and not put off by her reaction he grinned back. 'We all give off vibes, you know. Yours are placid, though at the moment they've gone haywire!'

'And Sophie's?' Erica could not forbear asking.

'They are haywire most of the time! That's why we get on with each other. She lifts me up and I calm her down.'

'Do you *believe* what you're saying?'

'Of course. I am simplifying it for you,' he admitted. 'You would find it easier to accept if you knew the whole philosophy behind it.' He folded his arms across his chest. 'I'm sorry Sophie chose to get you involved in our affairs. I keep telling her to relax and let things take their course, but she finds it hard to believe that things will move without her pushing them!'

'What course do you think events will take? Don't answer me if it's too personal,' she added hastily.

'I don't believe in secrets, Erica.' He used her name with ease, as though it never entered his mind to call her anything else.

It made her realize how much more thought Filippo Rosetti had given to it. His use of her name had been deliberate, his tongue moving over the word slowly as though he were savouring each vowel and consonant. How intimate he had made the name sound. She clasped her hands tightly on her lap and concentrated on the young man opposite.

'Sophie and I are in love,' he said. 'But I'm not sure if she will be able to accept me as I am. To live with me, she will have to follow my way of life.'

'*You* can't change, of course,' Erica said with faint sarcasm.

'I've spent the last three years changing. It isn't easy for a Westerner to adopt the philosophy of the East, particularly if he intends to return and live in a western culture.'

'Why are you returning, then?'

'Good things don't need to remain in the East,' he replied. 'Anyway, because I like their philosophy doesn't mean I like their total way of life. I was born overlooking the Manchester Canal and my roots are still there!'

'Do you see Sophie's roots growing there too?'

'It depends. I had no intention of falling in love with her, Erica. She isn't the sort of girl I had in mind when I thought in terms of my future. But I *did* fall in love with her, and I believe it was meant to happen.'

'Fate?'

'Karma,' he agreed.

'What do you have in mind?' Erica asked. 'She's under age, you know, and her uncle is very strict.'

'I don't intend us to live in sin! Nor do I intend to marry her yet. I must be sure she knows exactly what she's doing. That's why I would like us to be close together for the next year. But unfortunately I can't stay in Venice. I have a job to get back to.'

'I thought you were a perpetual mediator?'

'You mean the Count thinks so!' He chuckled. 'It's easy to be a holy man if you live like a hermit on top of a mountain! The crunch comes when you bring your ideas down with you into your everyday life. But that's what I'm going to do. As I've said, I'm not cut out to sit in the sun with my feet in the Ganges! I'm trying for the best of both worlds: Western technology allied to Eastern philosophy.'

'I wish you luck.'

'I'll need it.' He stroked his beard. His hands were strong and blunt-fingered. 'Sophie would like to live in London and be near me; that's why she tried to sell the brooch.'

'Was that at your suggestion?'

The blue eyes looked at her for so long that Erica felt her cheeks redden and wished she had left the question unsaid. 'That was an uncalled-for remark,' she apologized.

'It shows you have doubts about me,' he said matter-of-factly. 'I can understand that.' He folded his hands on the table and then began to rub the third finger of his right one. 'I'm getting a bump on the end. I suppose I should learn to use a typewriter?'

'I thought you were an engineer?'

'I write too.'

'You seem to do many things.'

'We are all capable of doing many things. It's a matter of learning to use one's energy. Most people fritter too much away in jealousy and fruitless ambition.'

'That sounds like a good tract. You should write it down!'

'I have. One day I'll send you a copy.' He stood up and with a soft good-bye, walked away.

It was easy to see why the Conte did not like him. In outlook they appeared to be diametrically opposed. The trappings of wealth and possessions meant nothing to David Gould and she was not at all sure how much meditation and philosophy meant to Filippo Rosetti. He seemed too confident to need any philosophy other than a belief in his own invincibility. It was a pity he had allowed himself to be put off by David Gould's unusual appearance. The young Englishman was far nicer than she had expected and was possessed of a sincerity she could not doubt. The Conte might see his easy manner as indolent, but she saw it as something much stronger and richer.

Sighing, she too left the table and wandered into the square. Alone in Venice on a Sunday afternoon. It was not the most pleasurable of happenings, and she vowed that next Sunday she would accept Johnny's invitation to spend it with him.

CHAPTER SIX

ON Monday morning it rained. The cobbled streets were treacherously slippery underfoot and the grey clouds lowered ominously over the gilded dome of St. Mark's. But it was oppressively warm and even in her light raincoat Erica was uncomfortably hot by the time she reached the shop.

As usual she opened it and as usual busied herself returning the more valuable pieces to the window. What was not usual was her mood of depression: it was as heavy and gloomy as the atmosphere and seemed far less likely to lift than the bad day. It would take more than a stiff breeze to blow away *her* black clouds!

In the event it only took a telephone call. Picking up the receiver in answer to its ring, she heard Filippo Rosetti's voice and nearly dropped it back on its cradle.

'*Buon giorno*, Erica,' he said calmly. 'I hope you enjoyed your evening?'

'I watched television and went to bed early.'

'Then you should be all set for a late night tonight.'

Disembodied, his voice sounded deep and more foreign. It also had a strange huskiness which, had she not known better, would have made her think he was nervous. Filippo Rosetti nervous because he was talking to an English shop assistant? The thought was too ludicrous to consider.

'You refused to come out with me last night because you believed my invitation only arose from our chance meeting,' he went on. 'But even *you* cannot say that my call this morning is an accidental one.'

'That remark of mine seems to have upset you,' she said.

'It has. I do not like to have my word or my intentions doubted; and you made it very clear that you doubted mine. Now then,' he said crisply, 'about tonight. If you are genuinely not free, I can make myself available tomorrow night instead. After that I will be in Rome for a week. Well, Erica, will you have dinner with me?'

'You make it impossible for me to refuse,' she said breathlessly.

'I will collect you at eight. Give me your address.'

She did so, and he repeated it to make sure he had it correctly, then said a quick good-bye and hung up. For a moment she continued to hold the receiver, not sure if she had dreamed the whole episode.

But at half past seven she was dressed and waiting for him, having already changed twice. Even now she was unhappy with her choice, but knew that no matter what she wore, she would never be wholly satisfied with anything she had in her wardrobe. Always she would see it through *his* critical eyes.

Nervously she wandered round the sitting room, her long skirts moving sinuously against her. The supple folds of green silk jersey were draped intricately around her breasts but fell in simple, flowing lines from the waist to her ankles. The bodice was cut lower than any she had yet worn, but the boutique owner from whom she had bought it had refused to alter it by a single inch.

'You have wonderful shoulders and skin, *signorina*, it would be a crime to cover them up.'

Looking at herself in the mirror, Erica conceded that the woman had been right, though she felt that the bareness called for a baroque necklace rather than the single strand of small pearls that she was wearing. Muttering, she took them off and put them away; it was better to leave her throat bare.

The dampness of the day had played such havoc with her hair that by the time she had arrived home it was hanging limply round her face. Thankful that shops in Italian tourist towns were always open late, she had rushed down to the hairdresser at the end of the alleyway and put herself into Albertina's capable hands, emerging an hour later with her hair gleaming silver-blonde from a herbal shampoo and sculpted round her face in a long, shining bob. Excitement had inexplicably made her paler, and she had applied rouge and lipstick with an unusually heavy hand. But now her own colour had returned, and she rubbed off the pink powder and applied a beige one.

She was trembling and sick from nerves, and hoped she had not made a fool of herself by accepting Conte Rosetti's invitation. For the hundredth time she tried to guess why he had asked her out, and for the hundredth time she came to no definite conclusion. If he wanted a girl to conquer, surely he would look for someone more amenable? Or did he harbour the illusion that she would be an easy conquest?

She peered through the window, but there was no sign of him and she drummed her fingers on the glass, her nervousness growing. Seeing her reflection in the window-pane, tall and slender as a votive candle, she wondered if he perhaps wanted a change from Claudia Medina's dark voluptuousness. Again she felt an upsurge of fear for what she might be letting herself in for, but before it could envelop her she saw his tall figure coming down the cobbled lane. Her heart pounded in her throat and she hurriedly looked round for handbag and mohair cape. She wanted to run downstairs and prevent him from coming up, but pride kept her where she was: she was not going to let him think she was ashamed of where she lived.

The bell chimed and she went to the door, forcing herself to walk slowly. She opened it and saw him on the threshold. All composure vanished and she shook as though with fever. What was there about this man that made her act like a schoolgirl with a crush instead of a moderately sophisticated young woman? It was more than his looks – though these were devastating enough to turn any woman's head – nor was it his sharp mind and astringent personality; rather it was an amalgam of all three plus a dash of some unknown magnetism. She searched for the right word, but the only one that came to mind was sex appeal. She inwardly smiled as she imagined his annoyance at being compared with a Hollywood film star. The Conte Filippo Rosetti considered himself far above that.

'You are ready?' he asked.

She nodded and, clutching her stole, followed him down the stone staircase, their steps echoing around them, and thence to the street where the night air was cooler but still damp.

'It is evenings like this that make me regret living in Venice,' he murmured. Seeing her puzzlement, he added: 'I would have liked to collect you in a covered car and deposit you in a restaurant instead of having to walk you through wet streets and protect you from dripping eaves.'

As he spoke he gave a flourish and produced a long black umbrella. Unable to stop herself, she giggled and he flashed her a smile in return.

'It is comical, is it not, to be collected by a man with an umbrella?'

'Not any man with an umbrella,' she laughed. 'But you are so definitely not the type to have one!'

'I agree with you.' He propelled her along the streets. 'Normally I leave my home by launch and make sure I only go to a restaurant that is a few paces from the Canal.'

'Don't you find this rather limiting?'

'I would if I lived here all the year round.'

'I thought you did.'

'I spend half the year in Rome.'

'In another palace?'

'Yes.' He saw no sarcasm in her question. 'But unlike my *palazzo* here, I do not occupy all of it: only the top floor which I have turned into a penthouse.'

'What's happened to the other part?'

'It is occupied by our insurance company and bank.'

'You seem to have everything worked out very well.'

'It was not always the case. My grandfather was like me – ninety per cent worker and ten per cent dilettante. But my father was the other way round, and when I came into my inheritance there were many things I had to make good.'

'How long has he been dead?' she asked curiously.

'Fifteen years.'

'You were very young to take on so much responsibility.'

'I was twenty.' His glance was sharp. 'Am I older than you thought?'

'I haven't given it any thought,' she lied.

He walked beside her in silence and she flung him a surreptitious glance. His profile was haughty and his mouth, seen from this angle, looked uncompromising and hard. They were walking under one of the arcades that bordered San Marco Square and he had closed his umbrella and was holding it disdainfully away from his side, looking for all the world as though he were going to drop it behind him at any moment. She bit back an impulse to tease him about it, not sure if he would appreciate being laughed at.

'What is amusing you, Erica? A dimple keeps coming and going in your cheek. Is it on account of me?'

'The umbrella,' she said impulsively. 'You're holding it as if it's going to catch fire!'

'I would like to consign it to one!'

She giggled. 'It's such a small price to pay for living in this beautiful city.'

His teeth flashed and he waggled the umbrella in her face. 'Perhaps I should learn to wear the English mackintosh!'

Before she could reply he caught her elbow and guided her into a dark courtyard. It belonged to a house, and he knocked on the green-painted door set into the heavy stone wall.

'You have not been here before.'

It was a statement, not a question, and she followed him inside, not knowing what to expect. Her first reaction was one of disappointment, for the room in which she found herself was plainly furnished, almost utilitarian. The walls were white, as were the cloths on the tables; the chairs were wooden and though they had arms they could not have been described as comfortable. Nearly every one was occupied: not with the élite, well-dressed people she had anticipated but with the soberly garbed customers all intent on eating. It was so unlike her idea of a smart restaurant that she was horrified to find tears in her eyes. Why had the Conte brought her to a place like this? Was he ashamed of his friends seeing her? There was no likelihood of their meeting anyone he knew here.

Unaware of her reaction, her escort signalled her to follow the waiter who was leading them to a table in a corner of the room. No sooner had they sat down than a bottle of champagne was placed beside them and foaming glasses set in front of them.

'To the loveliest woman in the room,' he said, raising his own.

She gave a quick glance round and he smiled.

'You do not think it much of a compliment, I see. I will have to say it later on, then it will hold more significance for you.'

Before she could ask him what he meant, a second waiter presented them with a menu: a deckle-edged card covered with copper-plate writing.

'Written daily by the *patrone*,' the Conte explained. 'You will permit me to order for you?'

She nodded and watched as he glanced at the card, pursed his lips and then rattled off his order.

'*Si, si*, Excellence.' With a flourish the waiter took the cards and disappeared.

'You were expecting something more elaborate, were you not?' Filippo Rosetti said suddenly, trapping her with his eyes.

'It isn't frightfully Venetian,' she admitted carefully.

'It is, however, frightfully good.'

She saw he was teasing and knew he had guessed her disappointment. If he could read her mind so easily, she must be careful what she thought.

'Tell me how you feel about the restaurant after the meal,' he continued. 'If you are still disappointed, then next time I will take you to Harry's Bar.'

She was suddenly happy at his use of the words 'next time', and even happier when he added:

83

'I thought you might have already been taken to Harry's Bar, and for our first evening together I wanted to take you somewhere different.'

He had certainly done that, she mused as she looked at the stolid citizens tucking into their plates of food. The French might be gourmets, but the Italians were undoubtedly gourmands.

Their first course was set in front of them and she saw the cream and coral of poached scallops floating on a bed of white wine. This was followed by a puff pastry pie filled with a combination of pasta and finely diced liver and chicken in a thick, aromatic sauce of mushrooms, basil, tomatoes and cream. It was the most delicious combination she had tasted: the puff pastry melted into tender flakes in her mouth, the pasta was rich with egg yolks and the minced meats proclaimed their farm freshness. Erica had two portions and though she felt too full to follow it with anything else, found it impossible to refuse the wild strawberries set before her as the final offering.

'Do you take back all your hard thoughts?' the Conte asked as, coffee cups in front of them, he leaned back and lit a small black cigar.

'It was the most superb meal I've ever had.'

'We will come here again and sample their lobster. Emilio has it flown direct from Ireland.'

'Irish lobster in Venice?'

'They are the best lobsters,' he said seriously. 'Even the French get them from there.'

'You are interested in so many different things,' she commented. 'Food, clothes, jewellery, your work.'

'Art too,' he added. 'My paintings were not all inherited. Quite a lot of them I bought.'

'Do you like possessing things.'

'I did when I was young. Now it seems fruitless. My main pleasure in owning beautiful things is to be able to share them with someone I love.'

'That shouldn't be difficult.'

'I said someone I love,' he replied. 'Not someone to whom

84

I make love.'

She flushed and stared down at her coffee cup. 'Is there any difference?'

'Do not be foolish,' he said softly. 'You must surely know there is all the difference in the world. I never knew quite how much myself, until recently.'

It would have been easy for Erica to read anything she wanted into his remark. She could see it as a declaration of love or a declaration of something more venal. Obviously it was the latter. But how skilfully he had made it. Knowing he was waiting for her to speak, she said the first thing that came into her head.

'I'm surprised you aren't married already. I am sure many women have been willing to oblige.'

'Many,' he agreed. 'But I have never met one whom I loved sufficiently to give up my freedom.'

'Not even for the sake of an heir?'

'I wish my son to have a mother whom I love with all my heart.' His eyes were dark and brooding, and despite the fact that they were sitting in a well-lit restaurant with people close by, he created the impression of being alone with her, as if his emotions were cloaking them from everyone else.

'You make love sound very significant,' she murmured.

'Do you not find it so?'

'I don't know. I've never been in love.'

'That answers my next question. I was going to ask why a beautiful girl like you is still single.'

'I don't consider myself beautiful.'

'Then you are blind! You are like a pearl. And one must look at a pearl with searching eyes in order to appreciate all it can offer. Hold it at a distance and all you can see is a round milky white object. But wear it against your skin and it takes on colour and warmth. It absorbs the radiance around it and gives it back to you with intensified richness.'

'You have an excellent line in compliments, Conte Rosetti.'

'I am being serious,' he said sharply. 'And will you please

85

be so good as to call me by my name.'

'I'll try,' she said, and concentrated on the last part of his sentence in an effort to forget the first.

'Do it now.' He slid forward in his chair and stared at her.

'Filippo,' she said coolly. 'It isn't hard to pronounce.'

'Your tongue rests on each vowel as if you were chewing an ice cube – and you give my name the same degree of warmth!' Elbows on the table, he leaned closer still. 'Say it with feeling, Erica, the way I say your name.' He repeated her name in a whisper, stressing the second syllable and giving it a foreign intonation. 'Now do the same for mine,' he commanded.

An imp of mischief that surprised her as much as it surprised him, made her utter his name in a languorously husky tone. 'Filippo ... Does that satisfy you?'

His eyes gleamed. 'I hope you learn other things as quickly!'

Scarlet-cheeked, she lowered her lashes.

'Let us go,' he said abruptly, and pushed back his chair.

No bill was given to him, though the proprietor appeared at his side to bow them out. The dampness had gone from the air and it was summery again. Draping her stole around her shoulders, she walked beside him. It had been a wonderful evening and she would remember it for a long time to come, even though it was difficult to know exactly what had made it so memorable; not their conversation, for that had been spasmodic and brittle; more for the atmosphere perhaps, and for her own tremulous awareness of him. Light-heartedly she had found him full of sex appeal, but she could no longer be light-hearted about it, and she was filled with a longing to throw herself into his arms, to have him hold her tightly and feel the touch of his hands ... She stumbled and he put his hand on her arm to steady her. He kept it there, making her even more conscious of his closeness and her own vulnerability. What on earth was happening to her? Was she allowing Signora Botelli's obvious awe of him to affect her own attitude? Certainly she had never before experienced nor enjoyed such male dominance.

Once again they were in a part of Venice she did not know well, but the muted sound of music coming from one of the houses prepared her for a night club, and she followed Filippo into a dimly lit vestibule that led into a flower-decked pavilion. A three-piece band throbbed soulfully into the night and a black-skinned singer did the same into a microphone.

Erica's earlier belief that Filippo was trying to hide his evening with her was dispelled as they edged their way towards a banquette some distance from the music, for at every step he was loudly and cheerily greeted by someone he knew. Even in the subdued light she recognized the flash of real jewellery and the cut of couture clothes. These were not people who would appreciate the subtle splendours of Emilio's table, though they were undoubtedly the kind who would recount to the world that Filippo had been seen escorting an unknown blonde. There was no question about it getting back to Signora Medina. Carrier pigeons would be used should the telephone give out! Didn't Filippo care if the woman knew he was dining with someone else, or wasn't it considered necessary to be faithful to one's mistress? The thought of Filippo alone with Claudia Medina made her burn with such jealousy that she searched for something cruel to say.

'I'm tired, Filippo. I'd like to go home.'

'We've only just arrived.'

'I didn't know you were going to take me dancing.'

'It's only eleven o'clock.'

'It might be early for you,' she replied, 'but *I* work for a living. I open the shop at half-past eight.'

'I work too,' he said, and pushed her down into the seat.

'I thought your work was keeping women happy,' she said pointedly.

His eyes glinted. 'Never more than one at a time, Erica. And tonight you are the one.'

'No,' she protested, and made to rise. But it was impossible for her to move; he was sitting close beside her and his long legs blocked her exit.

'Stay where you are and be quiet,' he said menacingly, then turned with a smile to greet the waiter who set the inevitable bottle of champagne in front of them.

'It's so phoney here,' she said vehemently, looking round with distaste. 'Everyone is shouting at the top of their voices and pretending to have fun.'

'They *are* having fun – and so will you if you stop working yourself into a rage about nothing. What have I done to upset you now?'

'I'm sorry, but—' She bit her lip and then plunged on. 'I just find the whole thing a pretence: your taking me out and flirting with me . . . the way you brought me here so that your friends could see us and – and—'

'Finish it,' he hissed.

'And report back to Signora Medina! Is that why you asked me out tonight – because you quarrelled with her? You said you only have one woman at a time and if—'

'Be quiet!' he ordered. 'If you go on like this I will hit you.'

'You wouldn't dare!'

'Don't try me.' He leaned close, his wide shoulders blocking out the room.

He went on staring into her face and the anger in her died, making her see the futility of her outburst and frightening her with the knowledge that she might have given herself away. He knew she was attracted to him – she was convinced of that – but he must never know how much. Never.

'I'm sorry, Filippo.' Her voice was ragged. 'I know you find my behaviour odd, but I – I'm not used to the continental way of doing things.'

'In what way are we different from the English?'

'In every way.'

'I think you mean in our attitude to love.'

She nodded, and knew she had to explain. 'Your marriages are often family arrangements and you see nothing

88

wrong in having a mistress. There are many other differences too.'

'Such as? Tell me, Erica, I am curious to know.'

'What's the point? You won't change and neither will I.' She stared past his shoulder at the dancers on the floor. 'Anyway, it doesn't matter if we have different opinions and values.'

'It matters very much indeed.' He pushed her further back against the wall by the hard pressure of his thigh. 'As you say, in some ways we are more prosaic about marriage than the English, but in other ways we are far more romantic. We appreciate the importance of marrying the right woman – and by that I mean someone who will fit into our family and our circle of friends. But once a man has chosen his woman he will remain with her for the rest of his life. No matter what other amours he might have, his wife and children will always come first. You will not find the deserted wives and children in Italy that you find in England and America! Some of our womenfolk may wish that their husbands were more amorous towards them, but they never have to wish for him to be a good father or a good provider. The Italian man is always *that*.' He rubbed the side of his face. 'As for our mistresses ... Here I find it difficult to answer you.'

'I thought you would,' she said drily.

'But only because you are so childish in your beliefs! Don't you think that some Englishmen also have other women? And do you find it impossible to believe that there are as many faithful Italian husbands as English ones?'

'I doubt it.'

'You speak from ignorance,' he said coldly. 'You will find more happy wives here than in your own home town! And do you know why? Because we don't leave them and spend hours in a public house or in a football stadium! We treat them as companions. We talk to them about our feelings, our ambitions, our sexual needs.'

'I knew you'd get around to sex!'

'Does sex frighten you?' he said savagely. 'Are you going

to spend your life as Sleeping Beauty waiting for an emasculated Prince Charming to lead you into a platonic marriage?'

'There's no need to be insulting!' she flared.

'Then why did you insult me? Or didn't you think I would object to being accused of bringing you here to spite Claudia? When I have a mistress,' he grated, 'I escort no one else until such time as I have left her.'

'Does that mean you've left Signora Medina?' Erica asked bluntly.

'One cannot give up what one has never had.' His thigh pressed harder against her. 'Claudia's husband was like an uncle to me. As a boy I was devoted to him, and when he died I felt it my duty to help his widow. Claudia was not left well provided, and I made it my business to put her affairs in order. But she herself has *not* been my affair. She is a friend: nothing more.'

'That isn't the impression she gives,' Erica said stiffly, remembering Signora Botelli's comments about the jewellery bills. 'You buy her things,' she added. 'She has come to our shop several times.'

'I buy her a few odd pieces,' he shrugged. 'So what? Money is relative, Erica. A few million lire means nothing to me. It costs me far more to have you look at me with contempt.'

'Don't talk like that,' she said swiftly.

'I am telling you the truth. From the moment I saw you I wanted to be with you.'

'You didn't give that impression.' Knowing she could not get up and run, she decided to do the only possible thing: confront him with his words and make him see it was useless for him to go on flirting with her. 'You didn't fall over yourself inviting me to have lunch with you, and you took another two weeks before you—'

'I told you I went abroad after the luncheon party. And the reason I waited a week before actually inviting you to the Palazzo was because . . .' He pulled at his lower lip. 'I will be honest and admit that I was fighting my feelings. I wanted to see if I could stop thinking about you.' He caught her hand, squeezing her fingers so tightly that she was hard put not to cry out. 'Do you think I wanted to fall in love with a frigid English girl who would look at me with contemptuous eyes and accuse me of having a mistress!'

'Now you *are* joking!'

'Only because I dare not be serious. If I am, I will disgrace myself by making violent love to you in front of half of Venice!' He jumped up. 'Come. You are right, we should not have come here. I will take you home.'

Not giving her a chance to speak, he bustled her out and walked her speedily along the quiet streets to her apartment house. Still in silence he escorted her up the steps to her front door, looking oddly out of place in the narrow hallway.

She opened her bag and fumbled for her key. Her fingers seemed all thumbs, but at last she found it and put it into the lock. It turned and she opened the door and then swung round to say good night to him.

'Oh no, you don't,' he muttered, and stepping inside, knocked the door shut with his foot and pulled her violently into his arms.

She tried to draw back, but he was too strong, and he pulled her closer still, so that her body was pressed tightly against his. She felt the warmth of him through the thin silk of her dress, and the heavy pounding of his heart as his arms squeezed her ribs.

'You're hurting me!' she cried.

'Then stop fighting me. I want you and you want me.'

'I don't!'

'You're lying. You do want me, Erica. I have seen it in your eyes all evening. You want me as much as I want you!'

He lowered his head and rested his mouth on hers. She kept her lips closed and was surprised when he did not try to force them apart, content instead to rub them gently.

'You have no need to be frightened of me, little one. I will never wittingly do anything to hurt you.'

'What about unwittingly?' she asked, and felt him draw back slightly, though not enough for her to escape his hold. 'We come from different worlds, Filippo – I know you deny it, but it's true – and because of that, we think differently. You won't be able to help hurting me.'

'You may hurt me too. What about that?'

'Could I hurt you?' she asked slowly. 'You are so strong and self-sufficient.'

He groaned. 'If only you knew how insufficient you have made me!'

Once more his lips were on hers and this time she did not stop herself from responding. Her arms went around his neck and the tenseness left her mouth and body. Feeling her relax, he gave a murmured endearment and then rained quick little kisses along her cheek and down the smooth line of her throat, coming to rest where a pulse beat in the delicate hollow beneath her collar-bone. His hand stroked the silky skin of her shoulder, his fingers as light as the touch of a butterfly's wing. She shivered and pressed closer still, feeling him tremble as she did so.

'Erica,' he said urgently, and tilted her face up until her mouth was just below his. His eyes were glazed and so dark that there was no difference between the pupil and the iris. Then the heavy lids lowered and his mouth came down to cover hers.

Desire and fear warred within her and fear won. Her hands moved away from his neck and clenched against his chest as she tried to push him away, at the same time twisting her head to escape his hungry demands. For an instant she thought he was not going to let her go, then he took his mouth from hers and released his tight hold.

'One day you will not be afraid of me,' he said huskily, and catching her hand, raised it to his lips. 'You are an innocent child pretending to be a grown-up young woman.' His eyes lowered to the curve of her breasts and then lifted again to meet her own. 'Sleep well, my little one, and think of me.'

Before she could collect her wits he had gone, and only as

she heard his steps swiftly descending the stairs did she run to the window and peer down into the street. She waited for him to turn and wave to her, but he did not look up. Instead he walked swiftly away, disappearing almost at once into the shadows.

Dejected, she turned back to the living room. It had been foolish of her to expect him to wave to her like a lovesick swain. He was too sophisticated to be bowled over by a few kisses, and though she knew he had desired her, she knew also that he could just as easily forget her when they were apart. Yet he had not spoken as if he wanted to forget her, nor as if their evening together had merely been a single, flirtatious interlude. He had gone out of his way to let her know that he felt they had a future together, though he had made no reference as to the terms of it.

She began to undress and, seeing herself in the wardrobe mirror, wondered what Filippo would think if he saw her now. Though slender and fine-boned, she was delicately curved, with small but tip-tilted breasts and a tiny waist curving out to smooth firm hips. She was as different from the average, well-endowed Italian girl as it was possible to be, and fleetingly wished for more obvious charms, thinking of Claudia Medina as she did so.

How adept the woman had been in insinuating an intimate relationship with Filippo, and how cunningly she had established her desire to please him; even to the extent of asking Erica to design long earrings for her to wear because Filippo liked to see her with her hair drawn back.

Had Filippo been speaking the truth when he said that Claudia was no more than a family friend, and that his care for her financial well-being stemmed only for his affection for her late husband? If this were untrue and he was lying, it could only be for one reason: to make her believe she was not usurping another woman's place nor stepping into a position still warm from someone else's occupancy.

Her cheeks burned at where her thoughts had taken her, and she hurriedly put on her nightdress and slipped between

93

the cool sheets. Would she see Filippo tomorrow? She knew he was going to Rome the day after. But when he had telephoned her today he had given her the option of seeing him tonight or tomorrow evening. Of course this didn't mean he was still free; he could well have made arrangements to see someone else. If only he had made some reference to it or said he would call her when he returned from Rome. But he had left without a word, only his dark eyes speaking a message that was open to so many interpretations that she was afraid to consider them. Perhaps it would be as well not to think of them at all; to take each event as it came.

Inexplicably David Gould came into her mind, and the reference he had made to fate bringing Sophie into his life. It was fate that had brought Sophie into her life too, for the girl's encounter with her in the shop had led to her meeting with Filippo.

Erica sighed and turned deeper into the pillow. Fate had not done badly so far, she mused; she might as well leave the rest to fate too.

CHAPTER SEVEN

FOR the whole of the next day Erica waited to hear from Filippo, and when he did not telephone her at the shop, she felt certain she would find a message from him waiting for her at her apartment. But there was no letter on the mat inside her front door and, still believing he would get in touch with her, she did not venture out again, but made herself an omelette and coffee which she took to eat on the small balcony outside her room.

Only as ten o'clock came and went did she admit he was not going to contact her that day, and she went to bed depressed by her disappointment. Tomorrow he was going to Rome and the earliest she could hear from him would be later in the afternoon. Even as she told herself this, she knew she was being childish; Filippo had no reason to call her and he was too much a man of the world to behave like a lovesick schoolboy. Yet though logic told her one thing, her heart led her to believe another.

'Stop kidding yourself,' she said aloud. 'Even if he's attracted to you, he won't let it interfere with his work.' Indeed this was exactly what frightened her. Filippo had such strength of character that he might well be able to compartmentalize his life and put her into one small section of it; whereas she had already made him the whole of hers. This knowledge made her see how vulnerable she had become, and how ready for love she must be if she could have fallen for this man so quickly.

'Am I in love with *him* or just in love with love?' she asked herself. 'Is it the magic of Venice that has made me so susceptible or would I love Filippo no matter where I had met him?'

She tried to visualize him with her father. How alien he would look with his impeccably cut clothes, his olive skin and jet black hair. But his breeding and manners would make him acceptable in any country; his sharpness of mind welcome at any dinner table.

Frightened at where her thoughts were taking her, she turned her face into the pillow and tried not to think of him lying in a magnificent bedroom in a *palazzo* less than half a mile away. Forget him, she told herself. He's probably already forgotten you.

Wednesday passed as slowly as Tuesday, made even more depressing by the knowledge that Filippo was now in Rome. In a determined effort to put him from her mind Erica set about making some jewellery designs and, trying to recollect the stones she had seen in the Rosetti Collection, worked out more simple settings for some of them. Though the workmanship of the antique pieces was breathtaking, they tended to detract from the jewels themselves, swamping rather than enhancing them. There was a lot to be said for replacing the gems for semi-precious ones: garnets instead of rubies, aquamarines and peridots instead of sapphires and emeralds. Such stones would look well in the hand-beaten gold settings, while the more expensive jewels could be set into simple uncluttered lines.

The emerald brooch which Filippo had shown her was an ideal example upon which to work, and she closed her eyes for an instant, then drew it on paper. She studied it for a while and began to evolve a new, more simplified design. Several hours went by before she was satisfied with what she had done, and she coloured it delicately to give a better indication of how it would finally look.

Signora Botelli was delighted when she saw it. 'I'd like to show it to the Conte Rosetti. Or perhaps we can leave it lying around when Signora Medina comes in. She has eyes like a lynx and is bound to notice it. If she told the Conte it would be less obvious than if *we* were to do so.'

'You'll get nothing from the Conte Rosetti that he isn't prepared to give,' Erica cautioned. 'He is a man who makes up his own mind.'

'I'm sure the right sort of woman can get around him. Men of strong passions have their weaknesses, and Claudia

Medina is *his*!'

Erica jumped up from her stool so quickly that she sent it flying; her precipitate movement was unusual enough to draw a searching glance from her employer.

'You haven't fallen in love with him yourself, have you?' the Signora demanded.

'Of course not,' Erica lied, glad she was bending down to pick up some jewel filings she had knocked to the floor. At least when she straightened she would have an excuse for her red face. 'He isn't my type. And anyway, if someone like Signora Medina appeals to him, *I* certainly wouldn't.'

'You have your own charm,' Signora Botelli replied. 'Many men would find your coolness and your shyness a challenge; particularly hot-blooded Latins.' The woman looked down at her plump hands, each finger beringed. 'Our men are in a class of their own. It is easy to fall in love with one. Remember that, Erica, and be careful.'

Erica sighed. How dismayed her kindly employer would be if she knew her warning had come too late. The fierce anticipation that each telephone ring brought her had left her in no doubt that she had already succumbed to Filippo's charms. She would never be able to chastise Sophie for falling in love heedlessly when she herself had done exactly the same. Yet she could not love Filippo deeply; she hardly knew him. What she felt was the excitement of the unattainable. One could only love truly when there was a meeting of minds and a similarity of background and outlook. It was impossible to love a man who had been born into a different world; whose social position and wealth put him as far out of her reach as a star. But though she said the words she could not make herself believe them. Her foolish heart had already made nonsense of her logical mind.

Friday was the hottest day of what Erica found to be the longest seeming week she had ever spent in her life. The air was heavy with the sultriness that spoke of a coming storm, and by the time lunch time came round she had a throbbing headache. At Signora Botelli's instigation she took an extra hour off and wandered past the stalls that bordered the

Grand Canal. Even tourist trivia – in the form of junk jewellery, dolls dressed as gondoliers and miniature gondolas in imitation silver and gold – looked better in Venice than anywhere else, and drew the attention of the crowds.

Because it was lunchtime there were not many craft moving on the water, though the cafés bordering the Grand Canal were doing their usual hectic trade. If every fried scampi eaten in this city were laid end to end they would probably reach to the moon and back!

The thought made her realize she was hungry, and she slipped down a side turning and made her way to one of the smaller *trattorias* which catered for the true Venetian. Here the accent was on food, with counters and stools taking the place of tables and chairs. She joined a queue of girls and young men and was soon standing by a counter near the open window with a heaped plate of fried seafood in front of her. She ate quickly, gratified that she was able to follow the conversation around her. Until she had come to live here she had spoken no Italian, but could now make herself understood without having to stop and search for a word.

It was only as she made her way back to the shop that it dawned on her that for the last few hours she had not even thought in English. It was a disconcerting realization and brought home to her the fact that she could not stay in Venice for ever. Reaching the arcade, she quickened her steps, though she was still some yards from the shop when she saw Signora Botelli standing outside the door waving in her direction. Afraid something was wrong, she began to run.

'What is it?' she panted as she came within earshot.

'The Conte Rosetti is calling you from Rome,' the Signora said agitatedly. 'Be quick!'

'Be quick?'

'*Si, si.* He has been hanging on the line for ten minutes. I said I expected you back at any time.'

As though on wings Erica sped into the shop and picked up the receiver, hoping against hope that she could keep the happiness out of her voice.

She must have succeeded, for their first exchange of conversation was banal in the extreme: pleasantries on the weather and a polite enquiry as to mutual health before Filippo impatiently broke through the fiction of restraint by suddenly exclaiming:

'I cannot wait to hold you in my arms! When am I going to see you?'

'I d-don't know,' she stammered. 'That depends on you.'

'It depends on *you*, *cara*.' His voice was like a caress and made her tingle from head to toe. 'Ask the Signora to give you the rest of the day off, and tomorrow too.'

'Are you coming back to Venice?' she asked quickly.

'No, but I am hoping you will come to Rome. Don't say you can't,' he said, cutting across the exact words she had been about to utter, 'because everything is arranged. Vincente – one of my servants – will come to your apartment to collect you in an hour and take you to the airport. I will be at the other end to meet you.'

'But I don't know if I can get the time off.'

'Don't be nonsensical!' His tone was crisp. 'Signora Botelli will not dare to refuse when she knows you are coming to *me*!'

'If she does – and I ignore her – I'll be out of a job.'

'I can occupy your time much better. Please, *cara*, don't make any more excuses.' His voice went low. 'Or is it that you don't want to see me again?'

She was speechless that he could even ask such a question, for her awareness of him was so strong that she was sure he must know it.

'Erica!' he said sharply. 'Are you still there?'

'Yes,' she said huskily. 'And ... and I *will* come. Oh, Filippo, I've never been in Rome!'

'I hope you are coming to see me – not the city.'

'You are the second reason,' she retorted, and heard him laugh before he said good-bye.

Not caring what Signora Botelli would make of her departure for Rome, Erica asked for permission to leave at once, and rushing back to her apartment packed a suitcase. Thank goodness she had brought herself some new clothes. She would take them all with her to save the trauma of having to decide what she might need. Only as she folded a filmy nightdress did she realize she did not know where she would be staying, and was struck by the invidious position in which she had put herself. Had Filippo invited her to Rome to try and seduce her? Equally important, would she have the strength of mind to resist him if he did? Hurriedly she snapped shut the lock of her case, then went to shower and change.

She was standing in the hallway, outwardly serene in blue linen with a cheeky scarlet straw hat and matching shoes when a wiry little Italian presented himself at the door. Explaining that the Conte Rosetti had detailed him to take her to the airport, he picked up her suitcase and darted down into the street and through several back alleys until they reached a white launch bobbing on the murky waters of a canal. Clambering aboard, she recognized the flag on the prow and felt her heart lurch at the thought of all the trouble Filippo had taken.

No sooner had she settled down than the launch zoomed out into the Grand Canal, keeping to the centre of the wide stretch of water. They went fast until the Canal veered right. Here there was far more traffic and their speed caused such a swell that several gondoliers shouted abuse at them as their boats smacked up and down in the water. Frightened that they might crash into one of them, Erica closed her eyes and did not open them until she felt all motion cease and knew they had reached the quayside.

Here a car and chauffeur waited to take her to the airport and the private jet that was ready to wing her to Rome. She had only flown infrequently and never before where she was the only passenger. Her mind boggled at the cost to Filippo of hiring this aircraft, though as she sat down and fastened her safety belt she saw that the ashtray placed on the table beside her bore the Rosetti crest. His own jet too! Somehow this brought home to her – more than anything else had done

– the great wealth at his command.

The thought of it was still subduing her when she crossed the tarmac at Rome airport and saw Filippo emerge from behind a barrier to greet her. He wore a dark suit, the material lightweight because of the heat, though its colour made him look more of a sober businessman and less of the idle aristocrat. He was paler than usual too, his heavy lids shadowed as though he had not slept well.

His greeting was punctilious, his words polite though his eyes said something different as he put his hand beneath her elbow and guided her to a waiting car. But even in its interior he did not unbend, and Erica glanced at the chauffeur's impassive back through the glass partition and wondered if this was the only reason for Filippo's aloofness. His coolness, coming on top of her own reassessment of his wealth, started to make her doubt her wisdom in coming here. All Filippo had needed to do was to beckon and she had come running like a puppy. She stirred miserably and put up her hand to smooth her hair, forgetting she was wearing a hat. The wisp of straw fell to the seat and Filippo looked at it and then at her.

'Don't wear a hat again, Erica. I like to see you with your hair free.'

She bit her lip, seeing the comment as criticism of her appearance. How positive he was in his likes and dislikes, and how regardless of the fact that by giving vent to them he might be hurting others.

'I like to wear a hat,' she said firmly, and slapped it on her head again.

Without a word he put out his hand and took it off.

'Give it back to me!' she cried, and reached for it.

Still holding it and still in silence, he pressed a button by the window. It glided down and he leaned forward, tossed out the hat and closed the window again.

Erica stared at him in consternation. He stared back at her: no longer tired, his face gleaming with triumph.

'How dare you!' she choked. 'That was my hat.'

'Not any more,' he said calmly.

His calmness was her undoing, and not even knowing she was so distressed, she burst into tears.

'Erica!' With a gasp he pulled her across the seat and into his arms. 'Darling, don't cry. Darling, I love you. Oh God, I love you so much.' He was kissing her now with a fervour she had expected from him when they had met at the airport, and holding her so tightly that she was powerless to move. 'I didn't want to hurt you,' he said against her lips, 'but I have been trying so hard to keep calm that I turned myself into ice. It was the only way to stop myself from melting all over you!'

'I thought you were disappointed in me when you saw me again,' she whispered.

With a groan he buried his face in her hair. 'I have been counting the hours until I could see you again, and once I knew you were on your way . . .'

He was unable to continue, but his hold and his touch spoke for him, and it was Erica herself who became aware of the chauffeur sitting only a yard away.

'Filippo, don't!' she protested, and pulled away from him.

'I will buy you another hat,' he announced in triumph. 'Something to make you look less of a schoolgirl.'

She stared at him helplessly. Any other man would have shied away from such a touchy subject, but Filippo had no such inhibitions.

'Do you always have to control everything around you?' she asked.

'Only if it interests me.' His eyes gleamed. 'And you interest me very much.'

It was an answer she could not quarrel with, and seeing the funny side of it too, she laughed. How hard it was to fight against a man like this; he could disarm a one-armed bandit!

He was speaking in Italian to the chauffeur, too rapidly for her to understand, though she realized what he had said when, some fifteen minutes later, they stopped outside a plate glass window in Rome's most elegant shopping thoroughfare.

'You weren't really serious about buying me another hat?' she expostulated.

'Having given yours to the motorway, the least I can do is to replace it!'

'You just want me to wear the things *you* like!' she retorted, and heard him laugh as he led her into the salon.

With surprising speed they re-emerged and the chauffeur deposited three hatboxes in the boot. Erica did not know when she would have a chance to wear such frivolous concoctions. Each one had cost a quite staggering amount of money, but her first instinctive protest had elicited such a cold stare from him that she had lapsed into silence, reminding herself that cost was relative and that the money he was expending on her meant nothing to him.

However when he ordered the car to stop outside a boutique her protest was too vigorous for him to gainsay it, and he signalled the chauffeur to drive on.

'It is cruel of you to deny me the pleasure of buying you a few trifles,' he murmured, catching hold of her hand.

'Don't rush me, Filippo. We hardly know each other.'

'But you came to Rome because I asked you.'

She blushed. 'I already feel guilty about that. I've never behaved like this before.'

'And you never will again – with anyone else.'

'Are you asking me or telling me?'

'Both.' He looked at her questioningly, but she turned and concentrated on the shops flashing by. Ahead she saw a commissionaire outside the gleaming glass and chrome entrance to a hotel, and she only realized this was where she was going to stay when the car drew alongside it and Filippo helped her out.

'There is plenty of room for you at my home, *cara*, but I knew you would be happier staying here.'

Only now did she admit to herself how afraid she had been of staying in his house, and the smile she gave him disclosed all her relief, making him shake his head and look at her with mischief.

'You see seduction behind every one of my actions!' he chided.

'I'm glad there isn't.'

'What makes you so sure?'

She coloured and purposefully went into the foyer.

'Everything is booked for you,' he murmured. 'I assume you would like to go to your room and unpack. I will send the car for you at seven. Wear something for dancing.'

'Would you like to come up with me and inspect my wardrobe?'

'I would like to come up with you.' As always he had the last word and she left him and went to the elevator.

The room he had booked for her turned out to be a palatial suite with bedroom, bathroom and sitting-room. Flowers were everywhere: long-stemmed cream roses, huge bowls of sweet peas and a basket of orchids on her bedside table. She did not need to look for any card. Only Filippo could have sent them. Burying her nose in the fragrant sweet peas, she stood for a moment unable to believe that all this was happening to her. But it was, and she must continually be on guard lest she lose her head completely. Yet how difficult it was whenever one of Filippo's gestures set it spinning.

Promptly at seven she was downstairs waiting for the car, feeling like Cinderella going to the ball. She hoped she was not too dressed up for the occasion, but Filippo's critical eye had put her on the defensive, and she was wearing the most expensive dress she had bought with her: a fluid tube of black crepe with no back to speak of and a minimal front held up by two narrow diamanté straps. Even Filippo couldn't expect them to be real diamonds, she thought with wry amusement as she adjusted the straps. Black made her look even more slender than she was and turned her hair to silver-gilt. The confidence she felt in her appearance put a spring into her step, as did the boldly admiring glances that followed her as she went towards the car that had drawn up at the entrance.

Only as she neared Filippo's home did it lessen, dropping

almost to zero as the Roman *palazzo* of the Rosetti family came in sight. It was larger and gaunter than the one in Venice, but once inside, she found the atmosphere palatial, and she crossed the inevitable marble entrance hall to the private elevator that would whisk her to the penthouse.

The lift moved upwards swiftly and she stepped out into another marble hall, this one in white and gold with an immense glass chandelier twinkling down on her from a blue and gold painted ceiling. A butler, not in livery as the Venetian servant but in a white jacket, led her through an arch to the living room.

It was a symphony in white and cream: white leather settees and armchairs, thick cream rugs on a black polished floor and steel tubular tables with black-topped glass to reflect the flowers massed on them. It was from the flowers and the paintings on the walls that the colour came. And what a riot of colour it was! Entranced she gazed at the Bonnard above the mantelshelf, the Dufy and Derain on either side of it, and the two Vlaminks on the opposite wall.

She had no time to see more, for Filippo was coming towards her, unbelievably handsome in a black dinner jacket. He held her at arm's length and studied her. It was a slow, deliberate appraisal, his eyes moving down the long slender length of her, pausing on the curve of her breasts before coming up to look into her eyes.

'You are more beautiful than ever tonight, Erica.'

'There must be *something* you can fault,' she teased.

He hesitated. 'The only thing wrong,' he said slowly, 'is that you do not look sufficiently loved.'

She gave a faint shrug, not understanding him.

'I don't mean "in love",' he explained, 'but loved. When a woman has given herself to the man she wants – when he has taken her – she has a certain luminous quality about her.'

'I don't believe it.' Erica was determined not to show her embarrassment.

'It is true,' he insisted. 'Soon you will find out for yourself.'

Her heart thumped and she took a quick step on to the terrace. It was some ten feet wide and forty feet long, running the entire length of the living room. Wicker settees and tables and a mass of greenery and flowers gave it the air of a garden, while the outdoor ambiance was further increased by a small fountain which played its sylvan tune beneath an arbour of roses. Below her lay the city of Rome, lights glinting in the blue dusk, its ancient ruins majestic in the gloom.

Filippo came to stand beside her. 'You will not always be able to run away from me when I embarrass you.'

Resolutely she stared ahead. 'I hope you won't always embarrass me.'

'I hope so too,' he murmured. 'Once you have been initiated into the art of love you—'

'Filippo!' She spun round on him crossly and he flung his head back and roared with laughter, then caught her hand and led her over to a settee.

Tentatively she smiled, still too aware of what he was implying to be completely relaxed with him.

'Come, little one,' he said, catching her hand. 'You will feel safer when we are among other people.'

The evening was an enchanted one. Filippo was everything she had dreamed a man could be. They dined leisurely at Alfredo's and then went on to a night club where he held her very close and sang snatches of love songs into her ear. He appeared to be as well known in Rome as in Venice, and many times couples came over to speak to him. He asked none of them to join him nor did he attempt to disengage his hand from Erica's, which he held tightly within his own.

It was two o'clock before he drove her back to her hotel, where his insistence that he see her safely up to her suite set her blood pounding through her veins. But his goodnight kiss outside the door was the essence of decorum, and to her chagrin she was deeply disappointed.

'There is no pleasing you, is there?' he called softly from the elevator. 'Would you like me to come back and show you what I would—'

'No!' she said with a laugh, and backing into the suite, closed the door.

On Saturday Filippo proved himself to be both considerate and understanding. Knowing she had never been to Rome he insisted on giving her a detailed tour of it, overriding her protestations that she would be happy to come to Rome by herself on another occasion for a sightseeing tour.

Armed with several books – which he frequently consulted – he took her round the Vatican City, seemingly as absorbed by its treasures as if he were seeing them for the first time in his life. They remained for a long while in the Sistine Chapel, eyes lifted to take in the overwhelming magnificence of the painted ceiling where men and angels played out their perpetual allegory.

'It's incredible to think of the effort Michelangelo put into this,' she murmured. 'All those years lying on his back on scaffolding, painting and painting.'

'Sometimes painting through the night,' Filippo added, 'because he couldn't bear to think of all the years he was wasting here, doing this,' he said, pointing to the brilliant ceiling, 'when all he wanted to do was to sculpt. So you see how unwillingly he created a masterpiece – one of the wonders of the world. And all at the command of a Pope.'

'But he *must* have painted from the heart,' Erica protested.

'No,' Filippo said emphatically. 'From his guts; from his strength. His heart was in marble, waiting to be hewn out and brought to life.' His dark eyes roamed the ceiling. 'Look at those red robes,' he whispered, 'and imagine them as Michelangelo's blood ... his life blood seeping away through the years that it took to create his homage to God.'

Reluctantly she did so, and the agony of the tormented genius who had worked here seemed to fill her.

'Now for lunch,' Filippo said practically, as if divining that she could take no more. 'And afterwards I promise you excitement without heartache.'

He was as good as his word, taking her to eat in a gay and noisy restaurant overlooking the city, and then driving her through the beautiful outskirts to show her the palatial homes of some of its wealthiest residents.

'I prefer your penthouse,' she commented. 'Though you have made it ultra-modern it still has the feel of the *palazzo* it used to be.'

'I think so too,' he agreed, and looked pleased with her for thinking the same.

It was well into the afternoon, and the sun was a deep orange ball in the sky, when they entered the ruins of the Colosseum. Filippo came to life as he strode around the arena, drawing an exciting word picture of the battles and orgies that had taken place here in Roman times.

'I can just see you watching the gladiators fight to their death,' she said, 'and placing bets on charioteer races.'

'Does that mean you see me as a bloodthirsty over-lord?'

'Very bloodthirsty,' she grinned, enjoying the fact that at last she could tease *him*.

'And what about *your* ancestors? Painting themselves with woad and whooping round in fright when my fore-bears came to bring them civilization?'

'Civilization! The world doesn't seem to have learned very much in a few thousand years. We're even more blood-thirsty now than we used to be.'

'More refined about it, though. It is no longer man against man but one group of technologists against another.'

'And one hydrogen bomb to destroy the world.'

'Stop being introspective,' he ordered. 'I'll give you a chance to throw some coins into the Trevi Fountain. Then you can wish for a better future.'

She did just that, but throwing in the coins he gave her, she wished instead for something more personal and wondered if he could guess what it was. But though his look was tender as she opened her eyes and saw him, he made no comment.

That evening they again went dancing and, as before, he

left her at her hotel suite, kissing her lightly on the forehead as he said goodnight.

Lying in bed musing on the events of the day, she was afraid that he regretted having asked her to spend the weekend with him. It seemed the only explanation for his almost platonic behaviour since they had driven from the airport. He had kissed her then with an aching longing that he had not shown since. Perhaps he had discovered that he was no longer interested in her; that the girl who had intrigued him for one evening in Venice no longer had the power to do so in the bright lights of Rome.

Restlessly she tossed and turned, eventually leaving her bed to stand by the window. Was Filippo asleep or was he too lying awake and regretting his invitation to her? She thought of the way he had acted towards her tonight: attentive and kind, holding her close as they had danced yet saying nothing that no one else could not have overheard. If he was detached tomorrow she would ask to go back to Venice in the afternoon. Since he had his own plane it would present no problem to him. She could even suggest returning in the morning. She sighed. She was not seeing him until lunchtime for he had a business meeting until then, informing her – as he had seen her surprise that he should be working on a Sunday – that he was negotiating to buy an interest in an American bank and that the President of it wished to complete the discussions as speedily as possible.

'But my chauffeur will take you for a drive,' he had added. 'And he will bring you to the penthouse for lunch.'

Deciding that when she saw him at lunchtime, she would suggest leaving immediately afterwards, Erica went back to bed. But sleep was uneasy and she woke up several times with a sense of loss that made her frightened of the depths of her feelings for a man she still felt she hardly knew.

CHAPTER EIGHT

IN the morning Filippo was as good as his word. At nine-thirty the clerk at the reception desk rang to say her car was waiting for her whenever she was ready and, because she was unused to having a chauffeur at her disposal, she rushed through her breakfast, reluctant to keep him waiting.

She had mapped out an itinerary for the morning and she handed it to him as she reached the car. He looked at it and then took a sheet of paper from his pocket, explaining to her in broken English that the Conte had already given him instructions where to take her.

Erica glanced at the list. It was similar to her own and she decided it would be rude to ignore the trouble to which Filippo had evidently gone. Putting her own list back in her pocket, she climbed into the car.

Though she enjoyed her tour, all her thoughts were centred on Filippo, and her anxiety to be with him made it hard for her to concentrate on what she was seeing. How could any monument or church, no matter how ancient, stop her from forgetting the fear that was absorbing her?

'I've had enough sightseeing,' she informed the chauffeur. 'Take me to the Conte.'

'Is too hot to look-a-da ole buildings,' the man agreed. 'Much better to sit on terrace and relax in-a-da sunshine.'

Smiling agreement, she was nonetheless shaking with apprehension when she finally went up in the elevator to the penthouse. She was a few moments earlier than she had planned and she hoped he was not still busy or thought she had come here deliberately early in order to check up that he really was working. But when why should he think she wanted to check up on him?

Nerves were making her irrational, proving once again — if she needed proof — that she had allowed Filippo to destroy her logic as he could well destroy her future if he were not going to be a part of it. The knowledge staggered her and blindly she reached out and pressed the stop button, bringing the elevator to a halt. She couldn't go up to the apartment yet. She had to wait and take hold of herself. She must be crazy if she could even think in terms of a future with Filippo. She was as far out of his world as a star; not only in terms of wealth but of nationality and tradition. And these last two would count more with him than anything else. Even if he could for a single moment consider her as a part of his life, the fact that she was a foreigner would give him pause for thought. She knew this, indeed she had known it from the very beginning, though it had not stopped her from dreaming impossible dreams. And they were impossible. She must keep telling herself this. It was the only way she could hang on to her pride. No matter how much she attracted Filippo, he would never regard her as anything other than a passing infatuation. She should never have come here for the week-end. To be with him like this would only make it more difficult for her to forget him.

She set the lift in motion and stepped out into the penthouse with a fixed smile on her face. Filippo was in the hall waiting for her, his expression concerned.

'I thought the lift had got stuck,' he said abruptly. 'It suddenly stopped and when I pressed the emergency button nothing happened.'

'I stopped the lift myself. I wanted to – I wanted to put on some lipstick.'

His look was keen, but he said nothing as he led her into the sitting room. It was pristine fresh and the scent of flowers was strong.

'No cigar smoke?' she smiled.

'We were in my study.'

Annoyed for not guessing he must have more than one reception room, she accepted a drink from him and went on to the terrace as she sipped it.

He followed her. 'You are looking pale, Erica. Are you tired?'

'A little. It must be the heat.'

'You should be in Rome in July and August; then it can be unbearable.'

'How do *you* manage?'

'I have a house further out in the countryside. It is cooler there.'

Again she was annoyed at her naïvety. Naturally he would have a house in the hills and probably an apartment in Paris and London too!

'I keep forgetting how important and rich you are,' she said brightly.

'Being rich does not make one important.' Over the rim of his glass he was watching her. His lids were lowered and all that could be seen were two dark slits. 'You seem different this morning, *cara*, tense and nervous of me.'

'I am always nervous of you,' she said truthfully.

'But luckily it was not enough to stop you from coming to Rome when I invited you.'

'That's probably making me more nervous,' she confessed. 'I should never have come.'

'Why not?' He set his glass sharply on the table and came to stand beside her. 'What nonsense is this? You wanted to come as much as I wanted to have you.'

'Did you want to have me?' she whispered.

'Do you doubt it? Haven't I given you any proof?'

Proof of what? she longed to ask, but dared not do so lest it forced him to lie in order not to hurt her feelings.

'I have enjoyed myself very much,' she said, knowing the words were a *non sequitur*. 'But even glamorous week-ends must come to an end. I should be getting back.'

'There is no reason for you to leave until late tonight. I have arranged for you to go at nine o'clock. Someone will meet you in Venice to take you back to your apartment.'

'You might have told me,' she said sharply.

'I thought you would be happy to leave all the arrangements to me?'

'I do have a mind of my own, Filippo. I don't like you taking charge of me as if I were a child!'

'You're angry with me,' he said quietly, 'and I can see no

reason for it.' He caught her arm. 'I wish you to tell me why.'

She looked away from him and the pressure of his hand increased, warning her that he would not be fobbed off with another inconsequential reply. But she could not tell him the truth without disclosing her feelings. She looked into the living-room and for the first time noticed a beautiful marquetry bureau standing against the wall. Above it hung a Gauguin. It was from the Pont Aven period, in the luminous yellows and brilliant reds and greens which the artist had used at that time. If she needed anything to reinforce her belief in Filippo's position, she had it staring her in the face.

'I'm not angry with *you*,' she murmured. 'Only with myself. It was silly of me to pretend. I'm not the type to be anybody's mistress. Don't say you haven't asked me yet,' she added quickly. 'I know it was in your mind when we were in Venice.'

'That is true,' he said. 'I will not deny it.'

She had not needed his answer to confirm her suspicions, but hearing it added to her desolation. She forced herself to look at him but could not quite bring herself to meet his eyes. Instead she focused on his mouth. This was more painful and she looked at his forehead and saw a pulse beating on one side of it.

'It was foolish of me to have come to Rome,' she repeated. 'Some things are better left to the moonlight. It's hard for me to explain, but . . .'

'You have made yourself very clear.' His voice was harsh. 'You have no need to apologize about it. I am glad you have been honest with me.'

'Yes . . . well . . . it would never have worked.'

'It might have done in the beginning.'

'No!' she cried. 'Never! I couldn't have . . .' She averted her head and swallowed convulsively.

'Never?' he reiterated. 'You mean you find me so repulsive that you could not even consider me as a lover?' His words were as devoid of expression as his face, which remained dark and impassive. 'You did not give me that impression in Venice. Exactly the contrary, in fact. That is why I asked you here. But as you say, the moonlight can make fools of us. Spending an evening with a man is different from being with him for two whole days. I am too old for you, am I not? And too foreign and different in my ways?' His voice grew louder and a flush warmed his skin. 'You are no longer seeing me as the glamorous Count Rosetti but as an ordinary man – a not so young Italian!'

'No!' she burst out. 'That's not true.'

'It is. Don't bother to deny it: I do not want your kindness, Erica. I am well able to take the truth.'

Wordlessly she stared at him. If she were not so astonished by his misunderstanding of what she had said, she could almost have laughed at it. Did Filippo really believe she saw him as an ordinary man? As a not so young Italian who was too foreign for her?

'*I* am the one who is ordinary,' she said, knowing she had to give him back his pride. '*I* am the one who is different.'

'What are you trying to tell me?'

'That I didn't say what I did because you are too old for me. Nor does your being foreign stop me from – from . . . What I meant is that it makes it hard for me to understand you.'

'It certainly does!' His lids were raised and his eyes glittered like jet. 'You are a fool, Erica!'

Her head tilted angrily. 'So are you if you think I'd agree to – to —'

'I know exactly what you'll agree to!' he grated. 'And *my* only foolishness was in not realizing you were so busy trying to hide *your* feelings that you had no time to consider what mine were. But you don't need to pretend any longer.'

'Pretend about what?' she whispered.

'That you don't love me.' He paused as if waiting for her to deny it. When she did not do so, the glitter in his eyes intensified. 'No protestations? No outraged pride?

'What's the use?' she whispered shakily. 'Anyway, I've never been a good liar.'

'Then you do love me?' He made no attempt to hide his triumph. 'Say it, Erica. I want to hear you say it.'

This demand was too much for her and she stepped away from him. 'How much of a victory do you want?' she cried. 'If you know I love you, then you also know that it's hopeless. Putting it into words won't make any difference. I've already told you I can never be your mistress.'

'I'm not asking you to be. I have always known you would refuse.'

'Then why ... what ...'

Two strides brought him close to her and she was angry with herself for having come to rest by the wall, for now there was no way of escaping him.

'You are upset because I have been behaving strangely with you since you came to Rome,' he said. 'But you have completely misunderstood my reasons. I was attracted to you from the moment I saw you at Botelli's, and when you came to my home I was even more strongly aware of it. I tried to tell myself it was your fragile body and your long fair hair: that it was only physical, the need I had for you. Even our evening in Venice didn't make me alter that opinion, though it did confirm that I was losing my ability to keep you at arm's length. You see, I've never been under any illusion that you would let me be your lover. You carry your virginity ahead of you like a banner,' he said with a slight smile. 'No matter how deep my desire for you, it never made me foolish enough to imagine I could change your beliefs.'

Amazement at all he had said made it hard for her to see beyond the words to the future they might be implying. Besides, she was scared to think of the might-be's, for to do so could bring false hope and even greater disillusion.

'I was glad when I had to come to Rome,' he continued, 'and I deliberately did not allow myself to call you for the entire week. I wanted to see if I could forget you – and I tried,' he said loudly. 'I must be honest with you, Erica, I tried. I worked like a maniac each day and I played like a maniac each night.'

'I don't want to hear,' she said quickly.

'You must. I went out with some of the most beautiful women I knew. I was determined to find peace in other arms, to find a way of forgetting big grey eyes and a childish mouth. And I succeeded,' he said ruthlessly. 'I found women to excite me and fulfil me; to make me feel their master and —'

'Then why bother with me?' she cried.

'Because it didn't last! I had an hour of oblivion and twenty-three hours of hatred for myself. And each time it grew worse. Finally even the hour of oblivion wouldn't come. All I was left with was an aching despair that only you could satisfy.'

The words were dramatic and would never have been said by an Englishman. If only Filippo had not said them either, Erica thought brokenly, for the image they invoked was more than she could bear.

'Yes,' he went on remorselessly,'I made love again and again and again! But each time it was *your* face I kept seeing, *your* body I longed to hold.' He pressed against her. backing her up against the wall. His thighs were hard and unyielding and the desire she aroused in him could not be doubted.

'You don't know what power you have over me,' he said passionately. 'Nor are you fully aware of your own emotions. You still see things in a cloud of innocence.'

'I can't help being young,' she protested.

'I know, and that's why I feel I'm taking advantage of a child.'

'A child?' she cried, and unable to bear any more, pulled his head down till she could touch his lips.

With a murmur he pulled her away from the wall, but only in order to wrap his arms around her and to press her body against the length of his. She had never been held so close to another person, for the thin silk of Filippo's suit was no barrier. Her hands dropped away from his shoulders and came up beneath his jacket. His shirt was so fine it was like touching his skin and her fingertips moved over the fabric. He shuddered at her touch and the pressure of his lips increased, his kiss deepening.

Feeling her abandonment, he shuddered again and his hand came up along the spine to undo the zip of her dress. The bodice slipped down and his fingers moved over her smooth skin to curve round her breast. As he continued to caress her she began to tremble and feel an unexpected emptiness that clamoured to be filled.

'I love you,' she cried. 'I love you!'

With a convulsive movement he pulled away his hands and stepped back. 'Be careful of me,' he said thickly. 'I am only human.'

'So am I,' she murmured, and went to draw him closer again.

But he shook his head and placing his hand on her shoulder, gently but firmly turned her round. 'Let me do up your dress, Erica.'

Blushing, she remained quiescent as he pulled on the zip. She heard him give a sharp intake of breath and then he caught her back against him and slipped his hands inside her bodice to cup both her breasts. His touch was like a flame and she burned with desire; so sharp and intense was it that her knees threatened to give way and she would have fallen had his hold not tightened.

'Darling,' he groaned, and lowered his head till his mouth came to rest on the side of her throat. She tried to turn to face him, but the movement reminded him of his original intention and he lifted his hands away with a sharp gesture pulled up her zip. Only then did he allow her to swing round.

'Behave yourself,' he teased.

'You're making it easy for me to do so.'

'Then reciprocate, *cara mia*, and make it easy for *me*. Or have you decided you want to be my mistress after all?' His smile was sharp as he saw the colour come into her face, but when he spoke again it was to say that lunch was already waiting for them.

The dining room, like the salon, was ultra-modern, with steel and glass tables and chairs and walls of shining dark blue metal with an iridescent gleam. The food was superb, though she had no appetite and had to force herself to eat. Filippo too only toyed with the meal, and seemed relieved when they left the table to go and sit on the terrace.

'I have made no plans for the rest of the day,' he told her, drawing her down beside him on a hammock. 'I thought we would laze and relax, unless you would rather do something else?'

Erica could think of nothing she would like to do more than to sit close to Filippo. Her sigh of contentment must have given him his answer, for he leaned back and closed his eyes.

Slowly the time passed. The heat of the afternoon was intense though the tubs of greenery and miniature trees gave the illusion of a garden and some coolness. From far below there was the muted sound of traffic – even on a Sunday Rome was not silent – while above their heads in the distant blue came the infrequent drone of a jet. Erica closed her eyes. Her limbs were heavy and she was overcome with lethargy. She started to count the seconds; when she reached twenty she would open her eyes and sit up, otherwise she would fall asleep. Five ... six ... seven. Next to her she heard Felippo's even breathing. Eleven ... twelve ... Erica slept too.

When she awoke she found herself lying full length on the hammock, her feet up and her shoes off. She turned her head and saw Filippo sitting in a chair a few yards away.

'You should have woken me,' she protested. 'Have I been sleeping long?'

'Not very. But I was sleeping too, so you needn't look so guilty.' He turned round as a maid appeared with a trolley. On it was a pitcher of fruit and a delicate china teaset.

'Tea time already!' Erica exclaimed, and glanced at her watch. 'I've been asleep two hours! Really, darling, you should have told me.'

'And have you feel more guilty than you do already?' He

half smiled. 'You should learn, *cara mia,* that if one has anything unpleasant to say, it is less painful to say it by degrees.'

'I think that's much worse.' She looked at him speculatively. 'I can't see you being patient enough to take your time doing something unpleasant. I think you'd want to get it over and done with.'

'When I deal with men, yes, but not with the fairer sex.'

He pushed the trolley towards her and without being told she poured him a glass of fruit juice and herself a cup of tea. This was one difference that could easily be resolved. If only it were possible to overcome all their other differences so painlessly. She longed to say this to him, but a glance at his face told her his thoughts were miles away, and instead she sipped her tea in silence.

The evening passed as effortlessly as the afternoon. They stayed on the terrace until dusk when Filippo put on some music, only stopping it as they went in to supper. They both had more appetite and she was also able to take cognisance of her surroundings. Everything looked as if it had been made especially for this one home, with no expense spared. Even the silver cutlery had the Rosetti coat of arms and the same blue enamel design as the dining room walls. She wondered if Filippo took his heritage for granted or whether he ever gave thought to the luck which had made him the son of such an illustrious house. It would be interesting to know the history of his family and she determined to look up some reference books when she returned to Venice. The thought of leaving Filippo was a painful one and she felt her throat constrict.

'I'll soon have to leave for the airport,' she murmured.

'Not for a couple of hours yet. I will drive you there myself.'

It was only as she stood on the aluminium steps ready to board the jet that Filippo again caught her close.

'Don't work too hard while I'm away, Erica.'

'When are you coming back to Venice?'

'In a few days — I am not quite sure. I will let you know.' He gave her a little shake and pushed her upwards.

At the top of the steps she turned and waved good-bye, then hurried to her seat and looked at him through the window. He stood on the tarmac waving for a moment, then turned and walked away. As he did so, the jet slowly moved to its take-off position and within seconds they were airborne.

At midnight Erica was back in her own apartment. Looking round the small sitting room it was hard to believe that a few hours earlier she had been in Filippo's sumptuous one. How easily money could diminish distance and make travel a pleasure instead of a chore. With a jet of his own Filippo could commute from Rome to Venice daily. She wished he would do so now and hated the thought of not seeing him tomorrow.

'Filippo.' She spoke his name aloud, but it echoed forlornly around the room, leaving her more lonely for him than she had been before.

Expecting Signora Botelli's curiosity about her week-end in Rome, Erica was agreeably surprised when no questions were asked. It was only as she pondered on it that she realized the woman's silence stemmed not from lack of interest but from the awe with which she regarded Filippo. Did the Signora think she and Filippo were lovers? Even if she didn't, Erica felt sure the woman had not considered that there might be something more lasting between them. How surprised she would be when she learned the truth! Erica hugged the knowledge to herself, and went contentedly through the rest of the day, not even worrying when there was no call from Filippo.

On Tuesday she waited anxiously for the post, half expecting a letter from him. But there was nothing, nor was there a telephone call. It was not so easy to remain contented and though she did not feel anxiety, she was nonetheless sufficiently edgy to find it hard to relax.

On the way home she bumped into Johnny and, unwilling to stay alone in her apartment all evening, accepted his invitation to dinner.

'I thought we had a date for last Saturday,' he said as they munched their way through heaped plates of ravioli in a small bright restaurant near to the Opera House.

'I was in Rome for the week-end.' She was reluctant to say more and was glad when he did not question her about it, though he looked peeved when she refused to make another date with him.

'I'm not sure what I'll be doing for the rest of the week,' she apologized. 'Please let me take a raincheck on it.'

'I have no choice,' he smiled. 'Just don't forget me.'

But Erica had other things to think about, for Wednesday also passed without any word from Filippo. It was hard to go on finding excuses for his silence. The first and second day it could have stemmed from pressure of work, but she could see no reason why it should have prevented him from calling her today. Her reluctance to telephone him and see if anything was wrong showed her how much in awe of him she still was and made no sense of her belief that mutual love could eradicate fear.

But *was* it mutual love? Did Filippo feel for her what she felt for him? Of course he did. It had been implicit in the way he had held her; the way he had resolutely resisted her offer of surrender. But he had never spoken of their future. He had said he did not see her as his mistress, but he had not told her in what other way he saw her. Held close to his heart she had assumed it had been as his wife, but now, with distance and time between them, she was not so sure.

Doubts which she had thought dead proved only to have been dormant and rose like a phoenix to threaten her. Deliberately she went over everything he had said to her on the terrace last Sunday afternoon, but all she could recollect was what she herself had said. How clearly she had declared her love for him; how resolutely she had proclaimed her unwillingness to live in the background of his life and how honestly she had admitted that she did not believe he wanted her to hold any other place.

With a vehemence as strong as hers he had asserted that

he had never seen her living in the shadows. Yet though he had said how he did *not* see her, he had not explained how he *did*, and her own imagination had filled in the words he had left unstated.

She could see the picture with painful clarity. Soon after she had arrived in Rome Filippo had realized she would never agree to become his mistress, and because of this he had withdrawn from her. It was this withdrawal that had precipitated their discussion on the Sunday afternoon and had led him to say much more than he might otherwise have done.

Naïvely she had seen his desire for her as a declaration of love and had made no secret of her own love for him. But at no time had he been sufficiently carried away to ask her to become his wife. Perhaps he still believed – despite all he had said to the contrary – that in time he could make her change her mind and live with him.

She looked at the telephone on the counter: the silent hated telephone. If Filippo had not called her then his silence could mean something far worse: that he no longer even wished to try and seduce her. Why should he bother when there were so many women eager to give themselves to him?

It was an enormous effort to work through the rest of the afternoon and when she finally left the shop she was a mass of nerves. To meet Sophie and David Gould was the last thing in the world she wanted, but seeing them come towards her as she crossed San Marco Square there was no way – short of pretending to be blind – that she could avoid the encounter.

'We were on our way to see you,' David Gould said. 'I promised to let you read my thoughts on meditation.' He thrust a book at her. 'Here they are.'

Surprised, she stared at the book in her hands. The cover was shiny and the cellophane band on it was sealed. But turning it over she saw David Gould's face smiling at her from the back cover.

'You wrote this?' she asked.

'David only got the copies today,' Sophie interrupted with a rush. 'But it came out in London last week and has had sensational reviews. His publisher has already cabled him to come back to London. He's been asked to talk on T.V. shows, on the radio and—'

'Erica doesn't want to hear all about that,' David interrupted.

'But I do,' Erica replied, delighted for him.

'Then join us for supper,' he said, 'and I will give you the low-down on success and David Gould!'

Knowing it would be better to eat with this young couple than to be left alone with her own miserable thoughts, Erica went with them to an unpretentious restaurant where she learned that Sophie had not been exaggerating in her account of the furore caused by David's book. It was considered a *tour de force* in philosophical circles yet was couched in language simple enough to be understood by the layman.

'I've already been asked to write a sequel,' he admitted, 'and been offered a fantastic advance to keep me in style while I'm doing it.'

'Will you accept?' Erica asked.

'No. I don't want to alter the plans I've made for my future. If it did that, it would nullify the philosophy I'm trying to promote!'

'David's going to take the engineering job he's already got lined up,' Sophie put in, 'and I've persuaded Mother to take a flat in London for six months so that David and I can go on seeing each other.'

'My literary success has convinced Sophie's uncle that I'm not entirely unsuitable,' David murmured.

Erica swallowed convulsively. 'Is Filippo – is the Conte in Venice?'

'No, he's still in Rome,' Sophie replied. 'But Claudia went there yesterday and I asked her to give him a copy of David's book. When I telephoned my uncle this morning I told him he couldn't say a famous author wasn't a suitable boy-friend for me.' The girl giggled. 'You can imagine how well that remark went down! But at least he promised he wouldn't object to my continuing to see David.'

'That's as much of a climb-down as we can expect,' David said. 'Take things slowly, Sophie. The harder you push, the more resistance you'll find.'

Sophie flung him a grin and Erica was glad the two of them were too preoccupied with each other to pay much attention to her. The discovery that Claudia was in Rome with Filippo showed her how logical her earlier thoughts had been. Regardless of what Filippo had said about Claudia he was still seeing her. Erica's cheeks burned. She had made her jealousy of the Italian woman so clear that Filippo would never have seen her again had he not wanted to make his position quite clear.

Aware that David was now watching her, she forced herself to join in the conversation, but after an hour she was exhausted by the effort and glad when the time came to go.

'We'll see you before we move to London,' Sophie promised. 'I'll call you next week.'

'Fine,' Erica smiled, though she had no intention of seeing either of them again. She wanted nothing whatever to do with anyone associated with Filippo. It was the only way she would be able to forget him.

That night she did not sleep at all and at three in the morning she gave up trying and went into the sitting-room to work on some jewellery designs. Even doing this reminded her of the man she loved and she flung down her pencil in disgust. It was incredible that after knowing Filippo for such a short time he was already so much a part of her that she could not stop thinking of him.

Her intelligence told her that eventually his image would dim, but she knew that nothing would completely eradicate his memory. Like Mary Tudor, she too would have a name forever engraved upon her heart.

CHAPTER NINE

IT was a relief to see dawn brighten the sky and long before her usual time Erica was in the shop working at her jeweller's bench.

Signora Botelli arrived at mid-morning accompanied by a plain-clothes detective whom she always hired when she was bringing valuable jewellery from her workshop. She showed the pieces to Erica, but they were banal in design and relied for their customer appeal on the size of the stones rather than the beauty of the setting.

'You must hurry up and complete the sketches for Signora Medina,' the woman said. 'We must strike while the iron is hot.'

Uncomprehending, Erica looked blank.

'It is difficult to know how long the Conte will be interested in her,' the Signora explained. 'An affair like this can die quickly.'

'It might go from strength to strength,' Erica replied, marvelling that she could continue the conversation without giving herself away. It was almost as if she were trying to see how far she could go before reaching the end of her emotional tether. 'The Conte might marry her.'

The plump face was quizzical. 'You are in a better position to assess that than I am. After your week-end in Rome I naturally saw the end of Signora Medina's reign.'

Erica knew she went scarlet, but she made a superhuman attempt to ignore it. 'I went to Rome on a foolish impulse – as foolish and impulsive as the Conte's invitation. It meant nothing – and nothing happened!'

'You owe me no explanations.'

'I don't want you to jump to the wrong conclusions.'

'But you like the Conte, *si*? I will not believe you are unmoved by him?'

'I like him,' Erica said carefully, 'but no more than that. I could never let myself become – become involved with him.'

'You are extremely wise,' the Signora said firmly, so firmly that Erica wondered if the woman meant it or was saying it in order to be kind. Perhaps she also knew that Filippo had changed his mind.

'Men of the Conte's type,' the Signora continued, 'lead very sophisticated lives. They make excellent husbands on the material level, but emotionally they are always seeking excitement. After the first year they are rarely faithful.'

Would Filippo be one of the rare ones when he eventually married? The question came into Erica's mind, but she dismissed it immediately. She had to stop thinking of him. If she didn't, she would never be happy again.

'You look pale,' her employer commented. 'If we are not busy this afternoon you can leave early.'

'I'm not in any hurry to go home,' Erica protested. 'As a matter of fact I thought I would stay later this evening. I made a few sketches last night and I'd like to mould them in plasticine.'

The Signora nodded agreement, but at five o'clock she asked Erica to go to the Lido and deliver a package for her to the Excelsior Hotel.

'The boat ride will do you good, and you could even have a swim while you are there.'

Erica shook her head. 'It's weeks since I've been swimming. That shows you what a true Venetian I'm becoming! When I first came here to work I was sure I'd be on the beach every single moment I was free.'

'It is always like that,' the Signora smiled. 'But even so it will do you good to get some fresh air.' She finished wrapping a charm bracelet and handed it over. 'It is for Mrs. Linton, room 2438 at the Excelsior. I promised her I would have it ready for her to wear tonight. Take it now and do not bother to come back.'

It was less effort to accept Signora Botelli's well-meaning kindness than to go on protesting that she did not wish to be free. Erica put the package into her bag and set off for the Lido.

As she waited in the queue to buy a ticket for the water bus, she noticed that the Excelsior launch had pulled into the Gritti Palace entrance. She might as well cadge a lift back with them. Even if they were not yet ready to leave she could sit in the boat and watch the passing craft and people.

This was exactly what she had to do, for it was some fifteen minutes later before they slipped away from the hotel and shunted across the wide expanse of water towards the Lido. Going directly in the hotel's private launch she was saved the long walk to the hotel she would otherwise have had from the water bus.

As it was the heat was enervating and her hair clung limply to her forehead and lay in damp silvery tangles on the nape of her neck by the time she handed the package to the clerk at the reception desk. Then she wandered out on to the terrace. She regretted not bringing her swimming costume with her, for though the beach was crowded the water looked exciting and the pool even more so. But it was too late to do anything about it now and she set off to catch the bus.

The rush hour had already begun and there was a long queue of vociferous, shoving Italians whose antics to be first in line made her realize how well-behaved and quiet her own compatriots were by comparison.

Even the Italian eye for a pretty girl was blind during the fight to find a seat, and Erica was bruised and battered when she eventually found herself inside the bus, pressed against the window. She wished she had found the strength to fight for an upstairs seat instead of allowing herself to be jostled into this Turkish bath atmosphere. But she was stuck here for the whole of the journey and she rested her arm against the glass, aware of the fat woman on one side of her and the hard wall on the other.

Once they began to move a slight breeze came in through the open windows, dispelling the heavy smell of garlic and cheap scent. The water over which they glided was turned into molten gold by the setting sun and this colour was reflected in the sky, the horizon of which was edged in rose and purple. This was the time of day when Venice looked its most beautiful. The rays of the sunset bathed the statues in radiance and picked out the gilding on the carved stone walls. Wrought iron, delicate as spiders' webs, lay their dark tracery along the edges of the narrow windows that broke the flat surface of the houses and *palazzos,* while the faded tiled roofs glowed rose and red.

Erica was overcome by the beauty. At every hour of day and no matter how inclement the weather, Venice had a heart-catching quality found nowhere else in the world. It came not only from the romantic waterways and winding alleys, but from the buildings themselves which, even though most were crumbling into decay from damp and rising water, could still be numbered among the loveliest in the world. If cities could be likened to flowers, then Venice was a rose which, even dying, still gave evidence of its earlier lush magnificence.

The bus swung into the side of the Canal and slowed down as they approached a landing stage. It stopped; the rail was lifted and a mass of people got off, to be immediately replaced by another mass. In the mêlée Erica managed to find herself a seat and they moved off again.

Several gondolas were following their course. The slim gondoliers dipped their poles into the water and glanced neither to left nor right, intent only on balancing their craft. But the occupants – mostly tourists – were looking eagerly around them or trailing their hands in the water. Occasionally a motorboat shot past, eliciting disgruntled looks from the gondoliers who had to balance themselves more carefully as their boats bobbed like corks in the spume. One motorboat was even now drawing angry protests, for it came dangerously close to the bus itself, then zoomed off again only to slow down further on and double back on its course.

Idly Erica watched it, half amused by the audacity of the

driver and half irritated by his disregard of the other boats on the Canal. But then it looked the sort of launch to disregard every other, for it had the air of a cosseted woman, the brass on it gleaming as yellow as a peroxide blonde, its paintwork as bright as newly applied make-up. Even the driver was immaculate in a sharp white jacket and gold braided cap.

As she continued to watch him he turned his head to judge the distance from the bus and then came alongside them again. He was now directly opposite Erica and she saw his face pucker with concentration as he steered the launch on a parallel course. It spurted forward and the interior cabin came into view. Its windows were open and the curtains were drawn back to show the bright blue leather seats and the man who stood haughtily in the centre of the cabin staring with penetrating eyes at the crowds on the top deck of the bus.

She caught her breath, not sure if she was dreaming. What was Filippo doing here when she believed him to be in Rome? And why was he staring so intently along the deck? She shrank back in her seat, wishing there was somewhere more adequate for her to hide and knowing it was only a question of time before those dark piercing eyes found her. Tense, breathless, she waited, praying that the bus would increase speed and move out of range but knowing this would never happen.

Felippo's eyes were scanning the lower deck, his head moving inexorably in her direction. If she turned her head the other way and pretended to be talking to the woman next to her he might not notice her. Even as she went to do so she knew the futility of it. Her silvery blonde hair would give her away, glowing like a lighted torch among the black ones.

She drew a shuddering breath. It was pointless to avoid Filippo. If she managed to hide from him now he would only seek her out at her apartment. It was better for her to talk to him here and let him know she knew that Claudia had been with him in Rome. It would save him from bothering to make excuses for not having contacted her since she herself had left him. Five days of silence and now he was coming after her with the purposefulness of the Demon King. Was it guilty conscience that made him seek her out? Did he believe that if he explained his actions she would be less hurt? How dared he treat her in this high-handed fashion, bringing her to Rome and making love to her and then sending her away and turning to Claudia Medina!

Defiantly she faced the window. At the same moment he saw her. His eyes narrowed and his hand came up and beckoned. She went on staring at him and his gesture became more forceful, making it clear that he wanted her to get off at the next stop.

She hesitated and then nodded. Instantly he relaxed, though the motorboat maintained its parallel course, only slowing down as the bus veered in towards the next landing stage.

Hurriedly she threaded her way through the crowded aisle, pushed past the solid phalanx of people around the entrance and went down the gangplank and on to the quay.

Filippo's launch was parked a few yards behind, and bracing herself for the unpleasant meeting to come, she went towards it. He was standing on the prow and he reached out and gripped her arm as she came down the steps and lifted her bodily on to the deck.

'Filippo!' she exclaimed, but had no chance to say any more, for he half carried, half dragged her down the short flight of steps to the inner cabin.

He almost threw her in and with the same violent movements slammed the door and drew the blue curtains across the windows, blocking out the rose pink sunset and filling the cabin with purple gloom. Still in the same violent way he strode back to her and pulled her into his arms.

'It's no use,' he groaned. 'I'm too old for you, but I don't care. I can't face life without you!'

His arms were like steel bands around her, crushing the breath from her body. In a daze she listened to him, heard him murmur words of love, broken endearments, and all the while he held her as though he would never let her go, until finally he stopped speaking and with shaking hands pressed her head into the curve of neck and shoulder.

How well she fitted there and what a sense of peace it gave her. But she could not rest here; it was not her rightful place. She went to pull back, but his reaction was sharp and unexpected.

'No!' he cried fiercely. 'I won't let you go. You are mine. Mine! I'll never let you go again. These past days have been hell! You do not know what they did to me. But I had to give you time ... it wasn't fair to rush you – to force you into something you might regret.'

'Force me?' she whispered.

'The way I did in Rome. I swept you off your feet. I tried to blind you with my position and my wealth; with all the things I could give you. I knew I was taking advantage of your innocence, but I couldn't help it. I wanted you to be mine on any terms.'

'I don't understand,' she said huskily.

'I know you don't. And that's what made it worse. You were so trusting of me.' He held her away from him, but still kept his hands on her shoulders. 'I wanted you to fall in love with me and I did everything in my power to entice you. I even toyed with the idea of getting you drunk and seducing you. Then you would have had to marry me! But thank heavens my conscience stopped me from doing *that*. I had to let you make a free choice; to decide your future for yourself. That's why I didn't get in touch with you this week. I wanted you to have time to think things over, to see me clearly without the glamour that surrounds me.'

Tentatively she explored his words; beginning to understand the reason for his silence. 'Do you think it was your position that turned my head? That I cared about your money and your title? Do you think that's why I fell in love with you?'

'I am too old for you,' he said abruptly. 'You are an innocent child and you will be happier with a man of your own race.'

'Then leave me alone to find one!' Her voice was shaky, but she managed to get the words out. 'Don't give in to your infatuation, Filippo. I know you're susceptible to a pretty face and blonde hair, but I'm sure you'll soon find someone else to rhapsodize over.'

'Infatuation?' he echoed. 'Is that what you think it is? Haven't you heard one word I've said to you? Are you deaf, or don't you *want* to know? I love you, Erica! I love you and I cannot live without you. I want you to be my wife. For five days now I have fought against it – kept telling myself I'm the wrong man for you – but I can't fight it any longer. You have got to marry me. I will know no happiness until you do.'

'You don't need to order me to marry you,' she choked, and fell against him, laughing and crying at the same time. 'You fool,' she wept, 'don't you know it's what I've wanted from the moment I met you? But I thought *I* wasn't suitable ... that I was too young and inexperienced. I thought you'd grow tired of me.'

Her tears fell faster and he took out a handkerchief and wiped them away. 'I will never grow tired of you,' he whispered. 'For the rest of my life I will love you.'

'Then why didn't you call me after I left Rome? Why did you ask Claudia to stay with you?'

'She did *not* stay with me,' he said imperiously. 'She came to Rome to see her lawyer and naturally I took her out. As for my not calling you – I have already given you my reasons. I won't give them to you again, Erica. We have wasted too much time on words. Now it is time for action. You are going to marry me at once. Then you won't need to ask any more foolish questions.'

With a sigh she leaned close to him again. 'Five days without hearing from you and then you come after me as if you are crazy!'

'I am crazy! Crazy with love and jealousy.'

'You have no reason to be jealous. You're the only man I've ever loved. I thought I'd made that clear to you in

Rome?'

'I was scared to believe it. There is fourteen years' difference between us and each year has been like a hurdle that I was afraid to jump. But a week without you has shown me I must knock those hurdles down, I must make you forget those fourteen years.'

'There's nothing to forget,' she said truthfully. 'I felt you were out of my reach, but it had nothing to do with your age.' All her love for him was in her eyes and they glowed like pools of silver-grey. 'It was *my* age that seemed wrong. I'll never be as sophisticated as the women you're used to, Filippo, and I don't think I'll ever get accustomed to living a life of luxury, but—'

'You will live the life you want to live,' he said purposefully, 'so long as you live it with me.'

'Darling!' she cried, and the rest of her words were stifled as he took violent possession of her mouth.

There was no restraint in his kiss, no barrier to prevent him from showing her how much he wanted her. His hands were gentle but insistent on her body, moving down her back to rest on her hips and then glide up the smooth line of her stomach to her breasts. They swelled at his touch and she trembled and held on to him tightly, her mouth opening wider still like a flower to the dew. He was trembling as violently as she was and the eyes looking deep into hers were glazed with passion. She could feel his heart hammering against her ribs, feel the blood coursing through his veins and making his body throb against hers. Wave after wave of desire rocked her and she shivered and clung to him, crying his name over and over again.

'Erica, don't!' He caught her hands from his neck and brought them down to her side. His face was pale and beads of sweat dappled his forehead, making him look inexplicably vulnerable.

With another shiver she stepped back and collapsed on to the nearest seat.

'It isn't easy to fight, is it?' she whispered.

'It is the first time I have ever tried to do so,' he confessed, and as her head tilted sharply in his direction, added: 'See what a reformed character you are turning me into, my darling!'

'I'm glad one of us is strong,' she teased. 'I never knew until now how easy it was to lose one's control.'

'Thank goodness I am the first one to make you realize it.' He drew her hand to his lips and kissed the tips of her fingers, one by one. 'I intend to be the last one too. Be warned, Erica. There is no turning back for you now.'

'I never want to turn back. You were the one with doubts.'

'I have told you why I had them – why I am still afraid.'

'You mustn't be afraid,' she urged. 'You have no need to be. When Sophie told me Claudia was with you in Rome I nearly died of jealousy. Don't make me go through that again.'

'Never,' he promised and bending forward gently, kissed her brow. 'I have made my decision, and if I were forty years older than you instead of fourteen it would not stop me from making you mine.'

CHAPTER TEN

Now that the miracle had happened and Filippo had asked her to marry him, Erica was beset by doubts about the life that would be hers once she became the Contessa Rosetti. Erica Rayburn, a Countess! Wife of an Italian nobleman who could trace his lineage back to the fifteenth century. It was almost too unbelievable to be true.

Yet it *was* true. Filippo's eyes fixed on her, intent and adoring, told her so.

'You will return with me to the Palazzo,' he said. 'I want to tell my sister the news.'

'Must you? It's only just happened.'

'What does that have to do with it? We have no reason to wait. And you will wish to tell your father, will you not?'

'Of course, but . . . I haven't thought as far as that.'

'Then think now,' he said decisively. 'Do you wish to fly back and speak to him?'

'That won't be necessary. I'm not a child and I don't need to ask his permission.'

'My daughter would always have to ask *my* permission. Your age has nothing to do with it.'

'English people are different, Filippo. Families aren't as possessive as they are in Italy. They don't take family obligations so seriously.'

'Then they are to be pitied.'

His tone brooked no argument and she fell silent; not that she wanted to argue on this subject anyway, for she was half inclined to agree with him. There was no doubt there were disadvantages in having an over-paternalistic father, but these would be outweighed by the knowledge that he was always there to turn to when you needed him.

She thought of her own father, married for the second time and so immersed in his work that he had not cared when she had elected to continue living in Venice. He had never asked if she intended to return home, and though at the time she had considered his behaviour civilized, after six months of living among a tempestuous warm-hearted race she saw it as indicative of a limited loving capacity. She looked at the man close to her. There was no limit to Filippo's love and he had no reticence about showing it. The stiff upper lip and detached manner of the British aristocracy was as alien to him as porridge for his breakfast!

Smiling tremulously, she drew his hand to her throat and held it there, delighting in the feel of his strong fingers on her skin. 'I hope I won't let you down.'

'Let me down over what? You are my perfect woman, cara. You will never let me down.'

'Don't say that,' she pleaded. 'I might turn out to have feet of clay.'

'You have exquisite feet,' he whispered, and put his free hand on her knee, smiling as he felt her give a delicious shiver.

The launch stopped and she saw they had drawn up at the small quay that led to the side door of the Rosetti Palazzo. Together they went through the rose arbour and across the lush lawn – there was no shortage of water in Venice – and into the vast stone hall.

Up the stairs they went and entered the drawing-room. The windows were wide open to the Grand Canal and the last rays of the sun filtered through on to the stone floor and the magnificent rugs that covered it.

The Conte's sister was reading, but as she saw her brother lead Erica forward, his arm around her waist, she immediately flung her book aside and jumped up.

'So it's true what Sophie said? I never believed her!'

'You mean Sophie is more romantic than you?' Filippo teased.

'I mean I never dared to hope you would be so sensible!' Anna smiled at Erica. 'I'm so thrilled that Filippo has chosen you. You are just the sort of girl he needs.'

'Meek and mild?' her brother questioned.

'Calm and cool!' his sister retorted. 'And able to stand up for herself.'

'Most women can do that,' he said.

'Sometimes standing up for oneself means treading on others,' his sister replied, 'but I know Erica will never do that.'

It was not possible for Erica to doubt Anna Charters' welcome and she was delighted by it. If only she could be as sure of the other members of Filippo's family; those illustrious aunts and uncles of whom he spoke so lightly and those rich and sophisticated cousins with their yachts and jets.

Anna was still speaking. Her brother's news had excited her and she looked flushed. The colour and animation on her face gave indication of how pretty she must have been before the tragic death of her husband.

'We must give a party, Filippo, and introduce Erica to the family. We will open the ballroom – it's more than two years since we have used it – and we'll decorate the outside of the Palazzo too. Sergio will be delighted to bring out the bunting and the flags. He was telling me only the other day that they must all be taken out and ironed before the creases in them become permanent. You must give me a list of the guests you want to ask apart from the relatives.' She glanced at Erica. 'I am sure there will be lots of *your* friends and family too.'

'I shouldn't think any of my friends would fly over for a party,' Erica said doubtfully, 'but obviously my father and stepmother will.'

'Filippo's sure to charter some extra planes,' Anna replied. 'He always does when he gives a ball.'

Erica glanced at Filippo with unaccountable nervousness. 'Will you?'

'*Si*. As Anna says, it will be necessary. A jet to bring my guests from New York; another for London and two of my own small ones to do a bus stop service around Europe!'

For a split second Erica thought he was teasing her, but then she saw the seriousness on his face and knew that every word he said was the truth.

'I – I'm overwhelmed b-by it all,' she stammered. 'Hearing you talk so casually about jets and giving a ball makes me feel a real country bumpkin.'

'You will get used to it very quickly,' Anna assured her. 'It is being poor when you have been rich that's hard to learn. The other way around is easy! Just watch the way I organize things and you will soon be able to do the same. And once you are married it will be *your* job to arrange the parties.'

'I'll never be able to do it,' Erica stated positively.

'Filippo will show you. He adores showing people what to do!' The woman gave her brother a mischievous glance. 'Two orchestras, I think, and the Milanese caterers we used last time.'

'Excellent,' Filippo agreed. 'I will order the invitations first thing tomorrow. A thousand, I think. Perhaps twelve hundred to be on the safe side.'

'Twelve hundred people for an engagement party?' Erica could not believe she had heard correctly. 'But that's crazy!'

There was a moment of hushed silence, and frightened that she had hurt them both, she looked beseechingly from Filippo to Anna.

'We don't have such big engagement parties in England. I would be scared to death meeting so many people. Couldn't we just – couldn't we just stick to the family?'

'No,' Filippo said incisively. 'And the fears you are displaying do not please me. You are not a child, Erica. Why are you scared of meeting people?'

'I'm not scared – at least not in the way *you* mean. It's just that I'm ... well, overcome by it all.' She drew a deep breath and gave him another beseeching glance. 'I told you I wasn't like your friends ... that I'm not sophisticated and assured.'

'You are not blasée and hard-boiled,' he agreed at once. 'But neither are you a little schoolgirl. I have no wish to make you over into a woman of the world – had that been my intention I would have chosen to marry one, instead of you. But on the other hand I wish to have a *wife* by my side, not a frightened child! We will have our engagement party and you will enjoy it – once you have made up your mind that you will.'

Erica clasped her hands together, noting with surprise that they were shaking. Filippo was displaying a firmness that bordered on cruelty. He had promised to be understanding and not to force her into a life style she did not want, yet here he was doing exactly that!

'Erica.' His whispered her name and came to stand close beside her, his body blocking out the rest of the room. 'Are you afraid for the world to know I love you? Are you ashamed that *you* love *me*?'

Appalled by such a question, she stared at him. How could he think such a ridiculous thing? For all his talk of confidence he was as unsure of her as she was unsure of herself. But his fear came from the belief that she might not love him enough, while her fear came from the belief that she loved him too much to let him tie himself to someone who might not be able to fit into his highly sophisticated way of life.

'Of course I'm not ashamed of loving you,' she cried. 'I'm scared! I love you so much that I'm afraid I'll let you down. Give me time to get used to our engagement. Please, Filippo, let's wait a bit longer before we tell anyone.'

'You are speaking like this because you are still uncertain.' His voice was hard as was his expression.

'That's not true.' Erica knew she had to make him see her point of view, though it was difficult for her to do so when she longed to throw herself into his arms and say she would agree to do anything he wished. Yet she had to stand her ground. Hadn't Anna made some reference to being delighted that her brother had chosen someone who would know when and how to assert herself? The knowledge stiffened her resolution and she tilted her head defiantly.

'Once we are engaged we will be invited out continually. I am still nervous with you, Filippo, and I want to be alone with you more.' She put her hand on his arm and knew a sense of power as she felt a tremor run through him.

Defiance and strength of mind was not the best answer after all. Feminine ploys were much better. 'I adore you, my dearest,' she murmured, 'but you have so little understanding of me. Otherwise you wouldn't doubt what I feel for you. Our love is new for both of us. Let's have a chance to enjoy it quietly.'

His lids lowered, giving him a shuttered look that made it impossible to read his thoughts. But when he raised them his eyes were tender. 'You are right, *cara*. I am a fool for not realizing it myself. But we will not keep our secret longer than a fortnight.'

'But—'

'A fortnight,' he said in a voice that brooked no argument.

Accepting her victory, even though it would only be for a short time, she sank into the nearest armchair. Only as she relaxed did she realize her limbs were trembling. Her first disagreement with Filippo and she had won it. A small triumph but a triumph nonetheless. She was not foolish enough to believe she would have many such victories over him. She glanced at him, savouring his finely etched profile as he turned towards a side table and poured some drinks. Would she ever get used to the sight of him or would his nearness always make her feel as though she were made of jelly?

He came over and handed her a glass of champagne, toasting her with his eyes over the rim of it.

'Danny called you a little while ago.' Anna introduced the logical present into this magic moment. 'He said it was urgent that you called him back as soon as you could.'

'Then I had better do so.' Filippo bent, kissed the tip of Erica's nose and left the room.

'Don't let my brother intimidate you,' Anna said. 'And please don't have any doubts that he loves you.'

'I haven't – not at the moment – but I can't stop them haunting me when I'm alone. My whole life has been so different from his – from yours – that I didn't expect you to be so pleased.'

'You are a snob,' Anna said charmingly, and Erica was still exploring the truth of this comment when Filippo returned.

'There will be a month's delay in our sending the collection to America,' he explained. 'Apparently the museum housing it in San Francisco has problems with its insurance company. They will have to improve their security arrangements and this will take them several weeks.'

'What a pity,' Anna commiserated.

'The delay is unimportant,' he shrugged, and from his pocket withdrew a leather case and handed it to Erica. 'The emerald brooch,' he explained as she opened the lid. 'As the collection won't be leaving here for a month, you will have a chance to reset the centre stone. You said it was loose.'

Gingerly she examined it. She had never held anything so valuable. The emerald was flawless and large. It was worth at least fifty thousand pounds.

'I think you should get someone else to repair it,' she said nervously.

'Is it too difficult for you to do?'

'Of course not, but—'

'Then what's the problem?'

'It's so valuable. I'm afraid something will happen to it.'

'Since no one will know you have it,' Filippo said, 'no one will steal it from you.'

A gilt telephone beside Anna tinkled and she picked it up, listened for a few seconds and then glanced at her brother. 'Sergio says Claudia is coming through the garden. Do you wish to say you are in?'

Only for an instant did Filippo hesitate. His eyes slid to Erica and mischief glinted in them. 'Of course I am in to Claudia,' he replied calmly. 'I am – as the English are fond of saying – free, white and over twenty-one.'

'You are also trying to make me jealous,' Erica said with equal calm, 'but I have great faith in you, and since you have assured me that Signora Medina is only a family friend . . .'

141

'But she would like to be more,' he said wickedly.

'Stop it, Filippo,' said Anna, and changed the subject by tapping the telephone. 'We have a new intercom service in the Palazzo,' she said. 'It is much more practical than pushing a bell and waiting for a servant to come.'

'And easier on their feet too,' Erica replied.

Anna laughed, aware of the subtle reprimand in the words but not appearing to mind them.

The door opened and Claudia Medina glided in, elegant in deep blue trimmed with white. The smile on her face stiffened as she saw Erica, but it did not stop her advance on Filippo, who went forward to meet her, arms outstretched in welcome.

'Claudia!' he said affectionately. 'What a welcome surprise. I thought you were still in Rome?'

'Without you, Rome is hot and boring.'

'And with me?'

'It is hot and exciting!'

He chuckled and led her to a chair. 'You will be staying to dinner, of course?'

'Are you sure I am not in the way?' Claudia asked the question without emphasis, though the quick glance she shot in Erica's direction said what the words did not.

'You are one of the family,' Filippo replied. 'You are never in the way.'

'As you have a visitor here, I was not sure.'

'Erica came to look at a piece of jewellery,' Filippo said suavely. 'I have asked her to repair one of the brooches.' He inclined his head in Erica's direction. 'Show it to Claudia.'

Annoyed with herself for being jealous, though she knew she had only herself to blame for it, Erica gave a frigid smile and did as he asked.

Claudia held the brooch carefully. 'It is fabulous. What a colour!' She looked up. 'I didn't realize it was a perfect stone.'

'All our stones are,' Filippo said indifferently. 'That emerald is one of the finest in the world.'

'And Miss Rayburn is going to repair it for you?' Without waiting for an answer the woman looked at Erica. 'Aren't you afraid of working on such a valuable piece?'

'I'm petrified,' Erica admitted. 'I don't intend letting it out of my sight.'

Filippo took the brooch and wiped it with a silk handkerchief. He did it carefully and methodically and then put it back in its box and returned it to Erica.

'I think I'll chain myself to it,' she smiled. 'That's the only way I'll feel it's safe!'

As if deciding that enough time had been spent on the brooch, Claudia started to tell Anna about her stay in Rome. Every sentence included Filippo's name and he joined in the conversation, talking of people and places Erica did not know.

She knew he was deliberately excluding her and felt an urge to get up and kick him. But it was his way of showing her the invidiousness of her position. Announce our engagement, he was saying, and no one will dare to talk without making sure you are included in the conversation.

She stood up, intent on showing him that two could play the same game. 'I think I'll be going, Conte,' she said coolly. 'I have already taken up enough of your time.'

'But you will stay for dinner?' He had his back to Claudia and the look he gave Erica made it clear she dared not decline.

'Very well,' she said faintly, and resumed her seat.

At eight o'clock they sat down in the small dining room off the main one. This room overlooked the garden which was beautifully lit at night and drew attention to the pieces of sculpture set in it. From her seat nearest to the window Erica had an excellent view of a statue that looked remarkably like a Michelangelo, and knowing Filippo it probably was! Once more she found it difficult to believe that his illustrious family would soon be hers. The thought was so frightening that it robbed her of appetite and made it impossible for her to eat.

If Filippo noticed she only toyed with her food he gave no

sign of it and instead concentrated on Claudia, who blossomed beneath his attention, fluttering her long black lashes at him and looking at him with open invitation in her lovely dark eyes.

Erica sighed. Filippo might only see Claudia as the widow of a close friend, but there was no doubt that Claudia saw herself as a far more intimate part of the Rosetti family. How could he be so blind? Yet when it came to emotional intrigues men *were* blind.

Finally dinner was over and they returned to the drawing room. Anna pleaded tiredness and went to her room, and Erica felt Claudia's eyes on her and knew the woman was waiting for her to go as well. Though she had been eager to go before, she now had no intention of leaving Claudia alone with Filippo, and she continued to sit in her chair and pretend she could follow the extremely fast Italian conversation passing between the couple in front of her. If Filippo was intent on making her regret her refusal to disclose their engagement, he was undoubtedly succeeding. Yet this only increased her determination not to give in to him. For this reason it was not until an hour had passed that she stood up.

'Thank you for a delightful evening, Conte, but it is late and—'

'I will see you home,' he interrupted.

'There's no need for that, Filippo,' Claudia said at once. 'My launch is downstairs and I will be quite happy to take Miss Rayburn home.'

Erica glanced at Filippo and knew a sickening sense of disappointment when he nodded agreeably. What a beast he was! Her temper rose, but she held it under control hoping against hope that he would find some excuse for not letting her board Claudia's boat.

But he did no such thing and went down between the two women to the quay and helped them both to climb aboard.

'Are you free for lunch tomorrow?' Claudia asked him. 'My accountant is flying in from Milan and I would like him to talk to you.'

'I have already made arrangements to lunch with Erica,' Filippo replied and, seemingly unaware of the glitter in Claudia's eyes, gave Erica an unexpectedly warm smile. 'I will collect you at Botelli's at noon.'

She nodded, too happy to speak, and watched his tall figure recede into the darkness as the motor launch chugged them swiftly away.

'You have become very friendly with Filippo,' Claudia remarked. 'He is a naughty man, always flirting.'

'Not with me,' Erica said coldly.

'It is clever of you to keep your feet on the ground, Miss Rayburn. As long as you do that you won't get hurt. Filippo is thoughtless. He doesn't realise what a devastating impact he makes on poor feminine hearts.'

Claudia lapsed into silence and Erica allowed it to continue, not knowing what would be a safe topic of conversation between herself and this subtle-minded woman.

'Felippo must be delighted you are able to repair some of his jewellery. Aren't you afraid of taking away something so valuable?'

'Don't make me nervous about it,' Erica pleaded.

'I don't mean to,' Claudia smiled. 'But I do feel you should be extremely careful. Will it take you long to do?'

'A few hours, once I get started. One has to be careful working with an emerald. It's a stone that shatters easily.'

Claudia shuddered. 'How awful if it did! If it were me I'd put a bit of glue on the back and leave the emerald where it was!'

Erica smiled. 'It's a simple job really. I can't understand why Filippo didn't get it mended before.'

'Because he doesn't wear the jewellery himself!' Claudia laughed. 'Once he is married his wife will no doubt wear every piece, but until then he is taking the line of least resistance.' In the pallid glow of a passing lamp, the dark eyes glittered. 'Since when have you called him Filippo?'

'Since I was in Rome.'

Breath hissed between Claudia's lips and Erica regretted

her answer. But it was too late to withdraw it, for the woman was looking at her malevolently.

'I hadn't realized you were with him in Rome.'

'There isn't anything for you to realize, Signora.' Erica glanced round and was glad to see the Danieli Hotel looming ahead.

'If you could ask your driver to let me off here,' she said quickly, 'I'm very near my apartment.'

The woman gave the order and the launch slowed and stopped. Erica jumped out, said a quick goodnight and hurried away.

Claudia could not do her any harm, yet she was unable to rid herself of a feeling of fear. It persisted throughout the night, disturbing her sleep and giving her such vividly unpleasant dreams that she was glad when daylight came and she could get up and begin a new day.

Half-way through the morning Filippo telephoned to say he would not be able to take her to lunch as he had planned.

'Are you lunching with Claudia after all?' she asked before she could stop herself.

'Yes. She rang me a little while ago. It seems her affairs are in more of a mess than I had realized, and as I am one of her husband's executors I feel it is my duty to meet her accountant and talk to him.'

'She's just making an excuse to stop you from having lunch with me.'

He chuckled. 'You sound jealous, little one.'

'I am.'

'Then you know how to remedy it. Once our engagement is made public it will put paid to all the designing women who are after me.'

'You're not a bit conceited, are you?' she said sarcastically.

'I am extremely conceited,' he chuckled. 'And with good cause!'

Smiling unwillingly, she replaced the telephone and turned to go back to her work bench.

'That was the Conte Rosetti?' Signora Botelli inquired.

'Yes. He was – I was supposed to be having lunch with him, but he has to see Signora Medina's accountant.'

'Are you sure it is not an excuse? I do not wish you to be hurt, my child.'

Erica felt so guilty at causing the Signora unnecessary concern that she decided to tell her the truth. 'As a matter of fact I'd like you to—' She stopped as the door opened and a customer came in. Seeing it was going to be a long-drawn-out sale she gave a slight shrug and went back to her jeweller's bench.

She had already taken the emerald out and it lay gleaming green on a black velvet tray. Bereft of its centre stone the brooch was easy to repair and she was working on the claws when she felt someone standing behind her.

Looking round, she was surprised to see Claudia. 'Good afternoon, *signora*. Is there no one in the shop?'

'I came to see *you*,' Claudia said. 'I wondered if you had done the new designs you promised me. I meant to ask you last night, but I forgot.'

'I've sketched out a few ideas, but I'm not satisfied with them.'

'Can't you at least let me see them?'

Erica hesitated and then went over to the desk. As she did so Claudia bent to look at the brooch.

'So you have taken out the emerald. You would be wise not to let it out of your sight.'

'Don't worry,' Erica said grimly, 'I won't.' She bent over the bottom drawer and searched among her designs to find the ones she wanted. 'There you are,' she said, and held them out.

Claudia swung round from the jeweller's bench and took them. She studied them for several moments and then nodded. 'I like them very much indeed. Can you give me a price for doing the one with the diamonds and rubies?'

'You will have to ask Signora Botelli. I will work out the carats involved and the time estimated to make it up. Based on that the Signora will give you the cost.'

'Excellent.' Claudia looked at her watch. 'I must fly or else I will be late for my luncheon party.

She hurried out and Erica returned to the jeweller's bench. The brooch lay where she had left it. The claws must set harder before she replaced the emerald. She glanced at the stone on the velvet tray, then picked it up and peeped into the shop. The Signora was alone and Erica asked her to open the safe and put the emerald away in it until they returned from lunch.

'I assume you will not be making the Conte a charge for the repairs?' the woman asked casually.

'I hadn't thought about it,' Erica admitted. 'Naturally I wouldn't want to charge him. I will pay you myself for the time I spend on it.'

'Do not be silly. I merely wished to know if it was a labour of love.'

'Very much so,' Erica murmured, and seeing the twinkle in her employer's eyes, said: 'The Conte and I are engaged. It is still a secret, but I would like you to know.'

'I am delighted for you ... delighted! You will live in Venice, of course. It is wonderful news. We will have a special celebration lunch together at the Gritti Palace.'

Brooking no argument, Signora Botelli took Erica to lunch on the terrace of this most elegant of all hotels. The tables were full, but this did not deter the plump matron and within a moment a table was found for them overlooking the water.

'How on earth did you manage it?' Erica asked.

'A bribe! But *you*, my child, will just need to mention Conte Rosetti's name!'

Erica blushed. 'I can't believe it's happening to me.'

'Neither can I,' came the honest reply. 'The Conte undoubtedly loves you.'

'Yes, he does,' said Erica, and tried not to be bitter that he was lunching with Claudia. She could imagine them sitting opposite one another in the undoubtedly elegant surroundings of the woman's home. Did she live in a *palazzo* too or in one of the old but elegant apartments into which many of the larger homes had been turned? Either way it made no difference, for she was sure Claudia envisaged her own future in the Rosetti Palazzo. How angry she would be when she learned that all her scheming had come to naught. But for the moment she did not know it and still saw Erica as a shadow on her horizon rather than a positive threat.

Refusing to let thoughts of Claudia and Filippo spoil the luncheon she was being given, she forced her attention on to the well-dressed people around her. Half of them were tourists, the other half being wealthy Venetians or foreigners who lived here regularly for the summer months; not tourists in the proper sense of the word.

'Have you set the date of your wedding?' Signora Botelli asked.

'Not yet,' Erica said quickly. 'Only that we're having an engagement party in about a month. A very big one.'

'Then I am sure the wedding will be small. A family affair only – and very soon.'

'I still can't believe it's happening to me.'

'You are a lucky girl, Erica.'

'I know,' she said humbly.

'And the Conte is lucky too. He will have a beautiful and talented wife and – most important of all – one who he knows will love him for himself alone.'

Erica gulped, made maudlin by the sentiment, though this soon changed to laughter as Signora Botelli regaled her with tales of her customers.

'If I were to publish all the gossip I know,' the woman chuckled, 'I could make myself a fortune – but lose a business!'

'And you'd much rather have the business,' Erica stated.

'No question of it. The gossip I learn adds spice to my work, but it is the work which I enjoy most.'

It was later than usual when they returned to the shop. The claws of the Rosetti brooch had already set properly and the Signora opened the safe and gave Erica the

149

emerald.

Carefully she put it into position and set to work. Slowly each claw was repositioned and the emerald held firmly in place. Only then did Erica sit back with a sigh of relief, for the first time aware that her forehead was wet. She wiped her hand across and deciding she owed herself a treat, picked up the brooch and pinned it to her dress. It looked out of place on the simple cotton and she undid it and threaded it through a gold chain. She would see what it looked like as a necklet. She fastened it round her throat and pulled her dress away from her shoulders as she peered at herself in the small mirror that hung on the wall. Worn as a locket the brooch looked magnificent, the emerald glowing against her skin and its colour reflected in her eyes.

'You are more beautiful than the jewel,' a deep voice said, and she gasped and swung round.

Filippo was lounging negligently in the doorway, though there was nothing negligent about the look on his face as his eyes moved over her.

Hastily she pulled her dress into position, undid the pendant and placed it in its case before she handed it to him. 'It's ready for you.'

'Thank you, *cara*.' He slipped the case into his pocket. 'I have come to take you home with me.'

'I can't leave yet. I don't close the shop for another few hours.'

'You will leave now,' he said quietly. 'Signora Botelli has agreed.'

Something in his manner told Erica not to argue with him. Filippo had so far gone along with her desire to keep their engagement a secret, but she had the feeling he had reached the end of his tether. Fear and excitement stirred in her at the thought of Filippo in a temper. He would be magnificent.

'Well?' he said impatiently.

'I'm coming. I'll just say goodbye to the Signora.'

A few moments later they were strolling along the arcade. Music was being played in one of the cafés and the square itself was thronged with tourists, pigeons and peanut vendors.

'How I dislike Venice in the summer,' said Filippo. 'Still, if I had not broken my habit and stayed here for part of this season I would never have met you.'

'It might have been better if you hadn't.'

'Still full of doubts?' He caught hold of her hand. 'Are they doubts about me or about your own feelings?'

'*I* won't change,' she said quietly.

'Then why can't you believe the same about me?' He squeezed her fingers. 'When you are truly mine, you will not doubt me.'

'Do you think sex can solve all problems?'

'I think that you need my passion to make you become a woman in the full sense of the word. And when you are, you will have sufficient confidence in yourself to be sure of me.'

'And when the beauty fades?'

'Even a dying rose has loveliness. We will grow old and happy together, Erica – I promise you that.'

'Oh, Filippo!' Tears filled her eyes and she clutched at his hand. 'What a wonderful promise!'

They reached the far end of the square and threaded their way through a maze of streets and over several bridges until they reached the gardens of the Palazzo Rosetti, an oasis of green among the grey stone. The rays of the setting sun lent it an apricot cast, and gave green depths to the murky waters that lapped at its sides. It had an enchantment it would not hold in winter, when mist and greyness superseded colour and the sun remained lemon cool and distant in a cloudy sky.

Venice in the winter. Venice in the winter with Filippo. She hugged the knowledge close. Wherever they were she would be happy, even if it was the North Pole. I'd probably be happier with him in the North Pole, she mused, glancing briefly at his austere profile as he walked beside her to the massive front door. Away from civilization there would be nothing and no one to disturb him; most important of all, no other woman to command his attention and she could have him all to herself. But this was a pipe dream and she was foolish to think of it. She had to get used to sharing Filippo with his friends and family. She must come to terms with her jealousy, for unless she did it would spoil both their lives.

'Relax,' Filippo murmured, putting his hand on her arm. 'You're as tense as a nun about to take her final vows.'

She laughed nervously. 'That is exactly the opposite of what I will be doing!'

'Opposite?' His eyes glittered. 'How do you mean, the opposite? Do you not see your marriage vows as final ones?'

'No – yes. I mean, I wasn't thinking of that part of it. Not the vows. Just that the promises I'd be making would lead me into a very different life from those of a nun.'

Conscious of his black eyes on her, she felt herself reddening and, seeing her embarrassment, he gave a low triumphant laugh and gripped her fingers.

'I can't wait till you are mine,' he whispered. 'You will telephone your father tonight and ask him to fly out immediately. If not, we will fly to him. I have no intention of delaying our marriage any longer.'

'We aren't engaged yet – at least not officially.'

He gave an angry exclamation but said no more as they crossed the stone hall and walked upstairs to the vast salon. It was empty and, seeing her surprise, he smiled.

'Anna and Sophie are in Rome. They will be living in London for six months, as you are probably aware, so they have gone on a shopping expedition to equip themselves for the wilderness.'

'London isn't a wilderness,' she protested.

'Try explaining that to my sister,' he twinkled. 'As far as she is concerned, no city compares with Rome for clothes.'

'I didn't think she cared that much about fashion.'

As she spoke, Erica could not help feeling vaguely depressed. Even Anna, sensible though she seemed, still had outmoded ideas of luxurious living: rushing to Rome to equip herself with a wardrobe for living in London for six months, and probably spending more in a few days than the average person would earn in a year. She knew it was ridiculous to compare one person's life with another. Besides, in spending money, the Rosetti family were helping to keep many people in their jobs.

'Your thoughts are not pleasant,' Filippo interrupted them. 'You do not find us easy to understand, do you?'

'I understand you, but I don't always find it easy to agree with what you do.'

'What do I – what do *we* do that disturbs you?'

'Many things. The way you live – all the panoply and the retainers – the enormous amount you spend on things I consider unnecessary. Even Anna's rushing off to Rome . . . It's such a waste of money. I'm sure they have wardrobes stuffed with clothes.'

He was so long replying that she was afraid she had angered him. He had asked her a point blank question and she had answered him truthfully, but now she wondered if it had been wise. In accepting Filippo's love she was also accepting his way of life. How much more simply Ruth had put it to Naomi. Thy people shall be my people. Thy ways my ways.

'You are worrying needlessly, Erica.' Filippo was again speaking. 'When you are my wife you may live the way you wish.'

She sighed. 'I doubt if that would be possible. You will expect so much from me, Filippo, and I'm not sure I can cope.'

'What is this nonsense you're talking!'

He came close to her and she could feel the warmth of his body and his magnetism.

'I make no excuse for having an illustrious name,' he said quietly. 'Nor do I excuse my wealth, for it was come by honestly, with foresight and hard work. I may not be your idea of a businessman, but I run many concerns that take up much of my time. Don't be misled because I have many hours to spend with you.'

'I'm not,' she protested.

'You are. I can see it in your eyes. You resent my wealth and, even more, you resent that in marrying me you might become used to it!'

'I'll never get used to it.'

'You will,' he assured her, 'and you will also go to Rome to buy your clothes. And to Paris too!' Before she could reply he pulled her into his arms and buried his head in her hair. 'Why are we arguing in this foolish way? We love each other, and these little differences will not matter once we are married.'

Pressed close against him, the warmth of his neck beneath her lips, it was easy for her to agree with what he said. Yet still the doubt lingered.

'I could never enjoy an idle life,' she whispered.

'Then you will only have a night nurse for the children, and look after them yourself during the day when I am busy!'

His words took her by surprise and she pulled back and looked into his face. It held a teasing expression, but more besides: a promise of love and tenderness, of a shared and happy future.

'I hadn't thought of children,' she said slowly.

'But you wish for them?'

She saw the anxiety in his eyes and instantly nodded. 'Of course. I would like a family, Filippo, if you would have no objection.'

'Do you expect me to have?' With a grin he pulled her close again and for the next few moments neither of them spoke.

When sanity returned, Filippo led Erica to an armchair and gave her a drink. As if afraid that her proximity could disturb him, he stood himself several yards away and deliberately gave her an account of the work he did, as if to reassure her that what he had said before was true.

To begin with, Erica enjoyed watching him more than listening to him; thrilled to see him sitting opposite her, so handsome and so much a man of control. But gradually she began to concentrate on his words and soon became absorbed in the glimpse he was giving her of his business life. It certainly seemed to be complicated, with many different companies vying for his time.

'It's like being at the helm of a ship,' she remarked, when he finally lapsed into silence. 'You can't steer the boat without all the ratings doing their jobs, and they can't take the boat anywhere without you at the helm. I can see why you're never bored, Filippo.'

'You needn't be bored either. If you are not entirely satisfied by the bringing up of our family, then you must concentrate on your work as a jewellery designer.'

'Wouldn't you mind?'

'Not as long as you are free when I am free, and providing you will promise me that you will not desert me for an office.'

'I can make my office anywhere. I'm sure you can find an empty room for me here and fit it up with a jewellery bench and my equipment.'

He smiled. 'I will see you have a workroom in all of my homes. You will not be the first Italian Countess to become famous in a career. We have many women of illustrious names who have established themselves.'

'Mainly in couture,' she said.

'And in other professions too, though perhaps they are not as well known. It is fitting that as a Rosetti, with all the Rosetti jewels at your command, you should be engaged in designing and making other beautiful pieces.'

'I might expect you to buy them all,' she teased.

'Naturally I would expect to have first choice,' he said calmly.

She giggled. 'I believe you would. But be careful, darling, it might cost you a lot of money.'

'I like that,' he said quickly.

'That it might cost you a lot of money?'

'No,' he said with a slight shake of his head. 'That you called me darling and it came so naturally from your lips.' He made a move towards her, stopping as there was a knock at the door and a man came in.

'Danny!' Filippo exclaimed, and went towards him. 'It slipped my mind that you were arriving tonight.' He led him forward and introduced him to Erica. 'I think you have already met each other the first time you came to lunch.'

Erica remembered and nodded. This was the American who was responsible for organizing the showing of the Rosetti Collection in America.

'I hope you don't mind me barging in on you,' he was saying, 'but there are some last-minute details I want to check over on the insurance side.'

'These insurance companies are a nuisance,' Filippo said impatiently. 'If you had allowed my own insurance company to handle it—'

'You are already taking enough of a risk in letting the Collection be shown,' Danny interrupted, 'without taking on the insurance too.'

'You have assured me there *is* no risk,' Filippo said with a sharp smile.

'Oh, sure,' Danny said hastily. 'But I know you look on the jewellery as priceless from a family viewpoint.'

'I have only one priceless possession,' Filippo replied, and looked at Erica.

The American stopped, astounded. 'Do I offer my congratulations?' he asked hurriedly.

Filippo nodded. 'At the moment it is not official. We are waiting to tell Erica's father.'

'I won't say a word to anyone.' Danny glanced from Erica to his host. 'I wouldn't have barged in on you if I had known. If you'd like me to come back another time . . .'

'Not at all,' Filippo said and, moving over to an ornate gilded desk, took out some papers from the drawer. 'Here are all the clearances you wanted. I suggest you look at them and let me know tomorrow if there is anything else that is necessary.'

The American took the papers and glanced through them. 'I'll take them back to my hotel and study them, then I'll return and make a final check on the whole Collection. It's still being guarded, of course?'

'Of course. A round-the-clock watch.' Filippo put his hand in his pocket and took out the leather case which Erica had given him earlier. 'I have one piece with me,' he explained, holding it out to Danny. 'The stone was loose and it has been re-set.'

Danny took it and lifted the lid. 'Magnificent!' he murmured, and moved over to stand beside one of the table lamps. He turned the brooch round to look at the back, nodding as he saw the quality of the workmanship. Unexpectedly he took out a jeweller's eye piece and, fixing it to his eye, began to examine the brooch.

'There is no need to inspect it quite so closely, my friend,' Filippo said drily. 'I can assure you the emerald won't fall out now.'

The American went on looking at it, then slowly took out his eye-piece and slipped it into his pocket. 'I can see you still don't trust our security arrangements, Conte,' he said with an ironical smile.

'Why do you say that?' Filippo asked in surprise.

'Because of this.' Danny tapped the brooch. 'Taking out the real emerald and putting in a dud one doesn't indicate much faith in us.' He glanced at the emerald again and then at Filippo, who was looking at him in utter silence. 'I can see I have surprised you, Conte,' he continued with a slight smile. 'I guess you didn't know I was an expert in jewellery, but you don't get to handle the stuff I have to handle without learning what's real and what isn't. Though this stone is a wonderful colour and expensive, I don't doubt, it isn't an emerald.'

Filippo was silent and there was something about the look on his face and Erica's too that told Danny his words had come as a total surprise.

'You mean you – you mean you didn't *know* the emerald's a fake?'

'No,' Filippo said quietly.

'It can't be!' Erica burst out. 'It never left my possession except to go into the safe, and I watched Signora Botelli put it there. The emerald can't be a fake. No one touched it except me.'

As she spoke she was aware of the American flinging a look at Filippo. 'We'd better call the police, Conte.'

'Not for the moment. Leave me to deal with this. If you will return to your hotel I will telephone you later.'

Danny looked as if he were going to protest. Then he thought better of it and silently hurried out.

As the door closed behind him Erica jumped up. She went to reach out for the brooch but before she could touch it, Filippo picked it up and snapped the case shut.

'Sit down, Erica,' he said, his eyes hard as jet. 'We have a few things to talk over.'

CHAPTER ELEVEN

EVEN months afterwards, when the troubled happenings were a thing of the past, Erica could never clearly remember the sequence of events that followed the discovery that the emerald was false. But she was glad that memory shrouded the horror which, even a long time later, could awaken her from her sleep in a cold sweat.

Alone in the vast drawing room Filippo made her tell him everything she had done with the brooch since he had given it to her to repair. But no matter how often she repeated her story, there was no discrepancy in it and no indication of where or how the real emerald could have been stolen and a fake one put in its place.

'It was never out of my sight,' she reiterated. 'Even when Signora Botelli put it in the safe, I was there.'

'Did *you* put it into the safe, or did she?'

'I did. The Signora unlocked the door, of course, but I put the emerald away, and then took it out again later.' She stared at Filippo. 'No one touched the brooch except me. I can't think what happened. Are you sure it was the real stone when you gave it to me? Perhaps the fake one was put in before you—'

'No,' he said heavily. 'Danny personally examined each piece – he was months doing it – and after every item was verified, it was sealed. I broke the seal of this box myself before I gave you the brooch.'

Erica's heart was pounding so loudly that Filippo seemed to be talking from a long way off. She could not believe this was happening to her. She blinked her eyes and shook her head, hoping the scene would change and she would find it had all been a dream. But Filippo remained standing quietly in front of her, while the brooch remained on the table, its green heart flashing. But not a real heart, she knew; an imitation one; a piece of green glass in place of a priceless jewel.

'You think I stole it, don't you?' she whispered. 'I'm the only person who had the chance.'

'Do not talk like a fool,' he said. 'You didn't do it.'

'Somebody did,' she said flatly.

'Not you.'

'Then who?'

'I don't know.'

He put his hand to his head. It was the first sign of indecision she had seen him make and it brought home to her the depths of his anguish. He wanted to believe her, of that she was sure, but logic was making it impossible for him to do so.

'You'd better call the police, Filippo.'

'No. I do not wish to cause a scandal.'

'You won't be able to avoid it. Questioning me yourself isn't going to bring back the emerald.'

'Do you think the police will have more luck?'

'They at least have more experience than you and—'

'You are right. I will call Vittorio. He's one of the men in charge. I can trust him to be discreet.'

Erica watched as Filippo dialled a number and spoke into the telephone. When he replaced it he looked more satisfied.

'He is coming over at once,' he said quietly, and went to stand by the fireplace. His face was so pale that his tan looked sallow. It emphasized the blackness of his eyes and his hair and made him look stark and menacing. Gone was the gentle lover she had always known and in his place was a man who was deliberately holding his doubts in check.

What would she think if she were in his position?

The answer was not a pleasant one and she realized how little he knew of her beyond what she had told him which, as far as he was concerned, could all have been a pack of lies. Yet even if he believed the story of her life, it still did not signify that she was the sort of person who would never be tempted to steal anything, no matter how great the provocation. Looking at herself with his eyes she saw only a frightened girl from an ordinary background who could well have decided that to be a Countess was too far out of her element for her to be happy. And if in seeing no future with the Rosetti family, she had finally succumbed to one of the Rosetti jewels ... She clasped her hands on her lap to still their trembling.

'I didn't take the emerald!' she cried. 'I swear it!'

Filippo took a step towards her, stopping as the door opened and a small, grizzled-haired man came in. 'Vittorio!' he breathed. 'Thank goodness you were in Venice.'

'If I hadn't been, I would have flown back.'

The two men greeted one another with warmth. Vittorio was totally unlike Erica's idea of a police inspector, being insignificant in appearance and almost overwhelmed by his shiny black uniform with its brilliantly polished leather boots and cap.

He set the cap on a table, bowed over Erica's hand as he was introduced to her and then perched on the edge of a chair as Filippo recounted what had happened. He did not interrupt once, though occasionally his eyes moved around the room, giving the impression that he wasn't listening. It was an unjustified impression, though, for as Filippo came to the end of the story, he began to question him minutely. Finally, satisfied that he had learned everything he could, he turned to Erica.

'From the begining, please, *signorina*,' he said quietly.

'Filippo has told you everything. I can't add to it.'

'I wish to hear it in *your* words. We will begin from the moment you took the brooch from the Palazzo.'

Erica searched back in her mind. 'When I got home I put the case under my pillow and—'

'How did you get home? Did the Conte take you or did you walk alone?'

'Signora Medina took me in her launch. But I don't see what that has to do with the—'

'I want to know *everything* you did,' the Inspector repeated. 'Every single detail.'

Failing to see how this was going to bring back the real emerald, she sighed and began again. 'I left the Palazzo with

Signora Medina. We both stayed on the deck of her launch and the brooch was in my handbag the whole time.'

'Did you open your bag for anything? To take out a handkerchief or a lipstick?'

'I only opened my bag to take out my front door key, and no one was with me when I did that. I was alone outside my apartment.'

'Inside the building?'

'Yes.'

Carefully the Inspector led her through the happenings of that night, not sparing her one single detail of what she had done. Many of his questions seemed pointless, but she forced herself to answer him. With so little to go on, every avenue had to be explored. Only as she came to the following day and started to tell him of the work she had done on the brooch did he allow her to tell her story without interruption. But he again insisted on minute detail when she came to the part where she had put the emerald in the safe and then withdrew it again after lunch.

'You were the only one to touch the stone?' he demanded. 'Your employer did not do so?'

'Only me,' she said, for the countless time.

'And before it was in the safe, where was it?'

'On a velvet tray beside me on the work bench. I left it on the tray when I put it in the safe. No one touched the emerald except me.'

'When you resoldered the claws how long did it take?'

'About twenty minutes. It might have been a bit longer. Signora Medina called to see me and I can't be sure of the time.'

'Does the Signora usually come into the office when you are working there?'

'She is a good client and comes in frequently.'

'Why did she come today?'

'She wanted to see some designs I had made.'

'And she looked at the brooch at the same time?'

'She already knew it,' Erica said with a faint smile and a glance at Filippo which he did not return. 'But she didn't touch it. No one touched it except me. It was never out of my sight,' she repeated. 'Never.'

'You sound as if you wish to be thought guilty, Miss Rayburn.'

'Of course I don't!' She was horrified. 'But I don't know how anyone could have—'

'You aren't *supposed* to know,' the inspector interrupted. 'That is why I have been called in. Now, please, you will answer my questions without any more interruptions.'

Once more he led her through the sequence of events that had taken place during Claudia's stay in the office, only pausing as they reached the point of Filippo's arrival at the shop to collect her and to take the brooch from her possession.

'What is the value of the emerald, Conte?' the Inspector inquired.

'At today's valuation, probably a million lire.'

Erica's gasp was audible and the Inspector stared at her. 'You did not realize it was so much?'

'No. If I had I would never have taken it to the shop. I would have brought my tools here. A million lire!' She put her hands to her head. 'I had no idea.'

'It won't be an easy stone to sell. Is that what you are thinking?' the inspector asked conversationally. 'Unless it is broken up into several smaller ones.'

'You can't break up an emerald the way you can a diamond.' Her reply was automatic, made without thinking. 'It would have to be sold as it was.'

'Would there be many buyers for such a jewel?'

'Many,' she said grimly. 'In Arabia alone you could find a hundred sheiks willing to pay that amount.'

'You speak with knowledge.'

The very lack of expression in the words made Erica realize the importance of their meaning. Too late she realized that her knowledge was implicating her, but knew that even if she had had warning, she would still have answered in the same way. 'I know my business, Inspector, as well as you know yours. My father is a connoisseur of antiquities —

Greek and Egyptian – and some of those are as valuable as anything in the Rosetti Collection. What applies to an Egyptian vase equally well applies to a jewel. But I did not take it.'

'That is what I am here to establish.' Black calf shoes gleamed as the man got to his feet. 'We will go to your apartment, please. I wish to look around.'

'Surely that isn't necessary.' Filippo spoke for the first time.

'I am afraid it is,' the Inspector said regretfully. 'But there is no need for you to accompany us. I can take Miss Rayburn myself.'

'Of course I will go with you.' Filippo moved to the door. 'Come, Erica. Let's get this horror over with.'

She was not sure what he meant, but his expression was impossible to read. In silence they went down the stairs, and as they reached the bottom one a bell pealed through the cavernous hall.

Filippo muttered inaudibly and they stood motionless as a liveried servant unlocked the door.

Looking at the figure who entered, Erica felt an enormous sense of desolation, as if a ghost were walking over her grave. Did Claudia Medina always know when to arrive at the most inopportune moment?

'Claudia!' Filippo went across to her. 'Is anything wrong? I wasn't expecting you tonight.'

'Anna said she had left a box of clothes for me and I came to collect them.'

'Clothes?'

'Old ones. For the charity stall at Princess Eda's garden party. You know I organize it each year. But if I am calling at an inopportune moment, I will come back when Anna is here.'

'No, no. I will have the box brought down for you at once.' Filippo spoke quickly, as if his mind was not on his words. 'Will you forgive me if we don't wait with you?'

'Is something wrong?' Claudia looked into his face. 'You seem disturbed.' The liquid brown eyes slid to Erica and there was a faint tightening of the lovely face. 'We always seem to be meeting each other here, Miss Rayburn. Have you come to repair some more jewellery?'

Erica drew a deep breath. She had half hoped Filippo would speak, that he would tell Claudia she was here because she was the woman he loved and was going to marry. But he said nothing, and with something like despair she wondered if he no longer wished to marry her. Perhaps he did think she had stolen the jewel. This could be the only reason for his silence.

Pride made her stare defiantly at Claudia. 'The emerald has been stolen.'

'Stolen!' Claudia looked at her in astonishment. 'But you had it this afternoon. I saw it.'

'You *saw* it?' Filippo asked.

'Of course. Surely Miss Rayburn told you? I went to the shop and she was working on it.'

'Ah yes. The emerald had been taken out of its setting, hadn't it?'

Claudia nodded. 'It was on a black velvet tray. I only saw it for a couple of seconds. I came to look at some designs Miss Rayburn had done for me, but I could tell she did not like me being in the office when she was working on the brooch, so I left.'

This was not quite the way Erica would have put it, but she forbore to say so.

'You only looked at the emerald for a few seconds?' Filippo repeated.

'Yes, my dear,' Claudia replied, and put her hand on his arm. 'I can see you are upset. I will come back for the clothes when Anna returns from Rome.'

Filippo nodded but did not disengage his arm from Claudia's as they walked through the garden to the jetty. Claudia's launch was moored there and he saw her down to it and watched her being driven away before he jumped into his own launch and guided Erica down.

His eyes looked into hers as she stepped on to the small deck, but she could not see any message in them, nor could she feel any warmth in the pressure of his hands as he steadied her as the launch moved down the canal. It could have been any hand on hers; not the hand of a man who loved her.

The living room of Erica's apartment appeared small with the Inspector and Filippo standing in it, and she was glad she had tidied it before leaving for work that morning.

'What do you wish to see?' she asked the Inspector.

'Everything. You will permit me to go though your things?'

'Is that necessary?' Filippo asked.

'You wish this matter to be cleared up, *no*? Then permit me to do it my way.' The man returned his gaze to Erica. 'I wish to examine everything, Miss Rayburn, but please do not be embarrassed. Regard me as you would a *medico* – a doctor.'

She shrugged and sat down, careful not to look at Filippo. But her tact was misplaced, for a sideways glance at him told her that his thoughts were miles away. How distasteful he must be finding all this. How sordid for Conte Filippo Carlo Marcello Rosetti, fifteenth of a line of illustrious aristocrats, to be sitting in the cramped quarters of his fiancée's home while her rooms were searched by a policeman who suspected her of being a thief! No wonder he was keeping his thoughts miles away! She would be lucky if he ever allowed them to return to her. She stared at the floor, trying to fight back her tears. She should never have become engaged to him. It had been crazy to believe they had a future together. Whoever had said that love conquered all could not have met this tall and arrogant Italian. There were some barriers that love could never overcome and the differences between herself and Filippo were insurmountable.

With a start she realized the Inspector was asking her to accompany him on his search and she went with him to the tiny kitchenette.

'I expect you'll want to look in the cereal boxes in case

I've hidden the emerald there! And don't forget the bread bin. I could have hidden it in a lump of dough.'

'Do not be angry, *signorina*. I am doing this in your interest as much as the Conte's.'

'I know,' she apologized. 'Forgive me, Inspector, but I am on edge.'

She returned to the living room and this time Filippo looked up. 'I'm sorry about all this,' she whispered. 'It must be awful for you.'

'I am the one who is sorry. I should have realized—'

She never knew what it was he meant to say, for he was stopped by a loud oath coming from her bedroom.

Then the inspector stood at the door, a shabby leather jewel case in his hand. It was one which her father had given her for her sixteenth birthday and she used it to keep the few pieces of jewellery she possessed, as well as some gemstones which she had started to collect as a hobby in the last few months. It was these stones that the inspector was now examining.

'Conte,' he whispered, and there was something in his voice which brought Filippo immediately to his side.

Erica saw them staring at the bottom of the box and the look on their faces brought her to stand beside them.

'What is it, Filippo? What have you found?'

Fleetingly he looked at her. Then his eyes returned to the leather case and, doing the same, she saw the jumble of gemstones lying there: a couple of rough amethysts, a piece of citrine, a lump of topaz, the pale yellow-green of a peridot and the deeper green of an emerald.

She caught her breath. There was no gemstone the exact colour of an emerald. She reached out for it, but the Inspector withdrew the case sharply, his expression hard.

'Do not touch it, Miss Rayburn.'

'Please show it to *me*,' Filippo commanded, and the Inspector held the case towards him. Filippo stared at the conglomeration of stones. 'It is the emerald,' he said, in a dull voice.

'It can't be!' Erica cried. 'It's impossible. Let me see it.'

Filippo took the case from the Inspector and lowered it so that she could look into its interior. Among the heap of rough-cut stones the large and beautiful emerald gleamed. There was no point denying what it was and no point denying she had taken it when it was here in her possession for everyone to see. Yet she could not accept a guilt that was not hers, and she lifted her head and looked into Filippo's face.

'I didn't take it. I swear to you I did not take it. Please, Filippo, believe—'

'Be silent!' he interrupted, and swung round to the Inspector. 'You will permit me to take the stone?'

'Normally we should keep it at police headquarters, but seeing its value and—'

'The fact that I called you in privately,' Filippo interrupted, 'means you will allow me to take it.' As he spoke he took out a clean handkerchief and lifted the emerald from the box, careful not to touch it with his fingers.

'Is it as fragile as all that?' the Inspector inquired.

Filippo's only answer was a shrug and he placed the emerald in his wallet. Then he looked at Erica. 'I have some things to do this evening. I suggest you remain in your apartment.'

She lowered her eyes. She could not blame him for believing her guilty yet, at the same time, he could have shown a little more disbelief. Not trusting herself to speak to him, she looked at the Inspector. 'Am I under arrest?'

The man glanced at Filippo and then his shoulders lifted in a shrug typical of the Latin. 'Not unless the Conte presses charges.'

'Come, Vittorio,' Filippo intervened, and strode to the door. 'Don't leave this apartment, Erica,' he said harshly. 'Not even in the morning.'

'But I have to go to work.'

'Very well, but don't go anywhere else. Nowhere else. Do you understand?'

She nodded, though she did not understand at all, and watched as he and the Inspector went down the hall. As they reached the stairs Filippo glanced back at her. His face was still colourless and his features were tight, making him look much older than he was. He hesitated, as though about to speak, but then the man at his side murmured something which Erica could not hear, and Filippo glanced at him and then followed him down the stairs without a backward look.

Erica closed the door of her apartment and returned to the sitting-room. She waited to experience the pain she knew she should be feeling, but no pain came. She was numb. Numb with a shock so intense that she could experience nothing. She sat in a chair in the centre of the room. Could this be happening to her, this horror that had turned her dreams into a nightmare?

'A nightmare.' She said the words aloud and pinched herself, hoping she would wake up and find it was nothing more than a too heavy dinner eaten close to bedtime. But though the skin on her hand turned an angry red, the horror of the moment did not abate and she knew it was real and lasting and not a figment of sleep. Only as the full realization of this dawned on her did the numbness recede and, like the blood returning to a cramped limb, the pain she felt began to increase in its intensity until she was unable to sit still and paced the room wildly.

Regardless of what Filippo and the inspector believed, she was innocent. That meant someone else had taken the emerald. Not only taken it, but planted it in her room in order to make her look guilty.

The knowledge that someone hated her enough to do this was as much a shock as knowing she was suspected of having taken it herself. But who hated her with such malevolence that they would resort to such an act? Filippo's sister might not have been pleased that her brother was marrying an ordinary English girl, but she would never resort to an act like this in order to discredit her. And Sophie certainly wouldn't have done so, nor David.

Could Signora Botelli have found it too much of a temptation to have the emerald on her premises and stolen it in a fit of madness? This made no sense either. The woman was old and extremely wealthy. To steal a jewel and run the risk of losing her reputation and business would have been foolhardy in the extreme. Yet greed made people foolhardy and the chance of possessing an emerald of such value might well blind one to the dangers of doing so. And planting it here would not have been difficult for her to do either, for it was the Signora who had found her this apartment and she might easily possess a key to it.

With a groan Erica put her hands to her head. It was crazy to suspect her employer. She would never have done it.

Yet someone had.

Only one other name was left, and because this was the person she disliked the most – and as such her obvious choice – she had refused to let herself consider it. Yet it was the only possible solution. Forcing herself to calmness, she tried to work out how it could have been done. No need to ask why; the answer was obvious. Merely how?

'I don't know.'

It was only as she heard the words ring out in the silence of the room that she realized she had said them aloud, and she repeated them again as if doing so would help her to find an answer.

But her mind remained blank. And she walked over to the window and stared out into the street. Small groups of people were moving along it and she realized that the hour was still early, though it seemed to her a lifetime ago since she had left Filippo's home. Again she went over everything she had told the inspector, but again she was no nearer finding a solution and she wondered if, after all, she was allowing her dislike of Claudia to cloud her judgment. Yet logic told her that of all the people she knew, this woman was the only one who had reason to dislike her sufficiently to want to do her harm. Rightly or wrongly, Claudia believed she had a future with Filippo; that given time he would ask her to be his wife. Seeing Filippo's interest in someone whom she regarded as inferior had been enough to arouse her jealousy, though the hatred had only come with the realization that the inferior English girl had been invited to spend a weekend with Filippo in Rome and – more frightening still – been brought to the Palazzo and introduced to his sister. Perhaps it was this gesture that had warned Claudia that Filippo's interest had been more than a passing one, for he was not the sort of man to introduce his casual affairs to his family. Yes, perhaps Claudia, coming to the Palazzo last night and seeing Erica looking so much at home there, had finally seen her as a danger to be destroyed.

Once more Erica paced the floor. She had a motive for Claudia's hatred, but she still did not know how the act had been done. She had never left Claudia alone in the office with the emerald. Carefully she went over the scene, forcing herself to recall every word spoken, every gesture made. Slowly it took more vivid form in her mind and she could visualize Claudia clearly, even smell the musky perfume the woman wore which surrounded her like a cloud every time she moved. But she hadn't moved very much after she had come into the office. She had just stood by the bench looking at the emerald and asking to see the designs that had been prepared for her.

Once again Erica relived that moment, but once again she could find nothing fresh to remember. She had shown Claudia the designs and soon afterwards the woman had left and she had put the designs back on the desk. No, she had put them back in the drawer, the lower one. No, that was wrong too. It had been the very bottom drawer of the desk. That meant she had to bend down to find them in the first place and for five seconds – perhaps longer – while she had searched among the papers – her line of vision had been blocked. But five seconds was more than enough time to pick up one stone and replace it with another.

Erica stopped her pacing. That was what had happened. She was as certain of it as she was certain of her love for Filippo. But not of his love for her. Quickly she pushed this thought aside. For the moment she must concentrate on clearing her name. Coming to terms with Filippo's lack of faith in her was something she would have plenty of time to do in the empty years ahead. And how empty those years would be. Tears filled her eyes and though she tried to blink them away, others replaced them and sent the first ones coursing down her cheeks to be followed by more and more until, blinded by them, she sank down and buried her head in her hands. What was the point of learning the truth if it couldn't bring back her happiness?

It was only a long time later when her storm of weeping had subsided that she again gave thought to her belief that Claudia was the thief. Having arrived at this conclusion, she wondered how it had been planned. She would have liked to believe it had been unpremeditated, for this would have indicated less hatred. Yet she knew it had been carefully worked out, for the false stone had not only been the same colour as the real one, but also identical in size.

Identical in size.

Horrified at where her conjectures had taken her, she longed desperately to share them with someone else. No one – no matter what they were willing to pay – could have found a stone to replace the Rosetti emerald without having it especially made. This meant that the action had been planned a long time ago and had not been done on the spur of the moment. If Claudia was indeed guilty, then she had been preparing her theft for weeks. Equally significant, it had nothing to do with her own association with Filippo. The woman's plan to implicate her had obviously been a spur of the moment – or more probably a spur of the evening – decision.

Curiously she pondered on what would have happened had she not taken the brooch away to mend. How could Claudia have made the switch unless she had anticipated being allowed to wear the brooch herself?

Erica's desire to tell Filippo all she believed was so strong that she ran to the window, half hoping to see him, yet not surprised when she did not. He was unlikely to come back and see her tonight. What was he doing? she wondered. Was he with the inspector, or had he returned alone to the

Palazzo? He might have gone to Danny's hotel to tell him the emerald had been found. She moved away from the window. Even if she saw Filippo how could she convince him Claudia was guilty when she had no proof other than her instinct?

The knowledge that she might never be able to prove her innocence suddenly hit her with overwhelming force, making her realize the priceless gift of having a good name. What a pity one did not appreciate its worth until one had lost it, she thought bitterly, and knew she had lost more than her name tonight. She had lost Filippo too, for even if he eventually believed in her innocence, she would never be able to forget he had doubted her.

'Filippo!' She cried his name aloud. 'If only you had more faith in me!'

CHAPTER TWELVE

ERICA was so reluctant to go to the shop the next morning that she almost didn't get out of bed. But her unwillingness to stay alone in the apartment was something that she disliked even more, and she forced herself to dress, drank a cup of black coffee and hurried down the street.

The beauty of the day was lost upon her, so intent was she on her own thoughts. Not that they were any more coherent than they had been the night before: hours of sleeplessness had still not brought her nearer a solution. She was certain Claudia alone had had the opportunity to steal the emerald but she knew she would never be able to prove it.

Casually she inquired of her neighbours on the ground floor if they had seen any visitor call on her, but the shake of their heads only confirmed her belief that Claudia had been too clever to allow herself to be seen. No doubt she had chosen the siesta hour during which to sneak into the building, and more than probably worn something unobtrusive in place of her usual elegant clothes. Even if she could find someone who would say they had seen a woman enter her apartment, she still had no way of proving who it had been.

Signora Botelli had already opened the shop when she arrived and was busy refilling the window. Aware of her employer's curious eyes upon her, Erica knew she was expected to recount further news about her engagement. But short of telling the Signora the truth – which she could not bear to do – she had to remain silent.

For the next hour she busied herself around the shop, dusting the counters, polishing parts of the glass where yesterday's clients had left their fingermarks, and then going into the inner office to sit at the desk and look at her designs. It was only as she did this that she knew she would have to tell Signora Botelli what had happened. If Filippo and the

Inspector judged her to be a thief, she could not expect the Signora to let her go on working here.

Before she could change her mind she jumped up and ran into the shop. 'I must talk with you, *signora*. I have something to tell you.'

'I have been waiting to hear it,' the woman beamed. 'The wedding day has been set, *si*?'

'No,' Erica corrected. 'It's over. Finished. He thinks I'm a thief . . . that I stole the emerald.'

In a rush most of the story came out, though she omitted her belief that Claudia was the guilty one.

'The emerald was found in your bedroom?' Signora Botelli gasped. 'But that is impossible! Someone has – how you say it in English – has framed you. You have been made to look guilty.'

'Filippo and the Inspector think I am.'

'*Stupido*! Not even an inspector of police can be such a fool! He has only to look into your face to see your innocence. I will go and talk to him at once – and the Conte too. They are both mad, mad!'

'You mustn't go and see them.' Agitated, Erica caught the Signora by the arm. 'It won't do any good.'

'It won't do any harm either for them to know I think they are crazy!' She burst into a spate of Italian, using an argot which Erica could not follow and which told her much more of the woman's original peasant background than could be guessed from her present rich and sophisticated position. Only when she had exhausted her temper at the stupidity of men did she lapse into English again.

'Who did it?' she asked abruptly. 'We know *you* didn't, so that means someone else did.'

Erica was so overwhelmed by the Signora's defence of her that she could have wept. Instead, she hugged the plump shoulders and stammered her thanks.

'Thank me later,' the Signora said brusquely. 'First we must work out how the real emerald was taken.'

'I think I know.'

'Then why haven't you—?'

'Because I can't prove it.' Quickly she recounted her suspicions, explaining not only how she thought the emerald had been substituted but also why.

'I think you have hit the hammer on the head,' said the Signora, her usual fluency in error. 'The only thing that puzzles me is where Signora Medina got such an exact replica made. She must have had it done in Rome or Milan. It would have been too dangerous to have gone to anyone here.'

'It must have been very expensive too,' Erica added. 'She obviously intended switching stones and selling the real one.'

'That means that even before *you* came on the scene she was not so sure of capturing the Conte as a husband.' Signora Botelli shook her head in amazement. 'She must hate you very much indeed, to have done such a thing. Not just to switch the jewels but to plant the real one in your apartment. She had to make *certain* you were known to be guilty.'

'A million lire worth of hate,' Erica sighed. 'It's frightening, isn't it?'

'But what if the Conte hadn't given you the brooch to mend? How would she have managed to make the change-over?'

'Perhaps she was hoping he would let her wear it one evening.'

'Of course. I think she may even have had a copy of the *whole* brooch made. Then she could have substituted the entire piece.'

Erica's admiration for the Signora grew. 'I never thought of that.'

'I would have made a better thief than you,' the woman said drily. 'It is the obvious solution. The entire brooch was going to be switched, but when she discovered you were going to re-set the emerald, she changed her plans in order to make you look guilty.'

Erica nodded. Everything was falling into place. But best of all she was pleased to think that Claudia had planned to steal the brooch a long time ago, for it meant Filippo had never indicated a desire to marry her.

'If she had changed one brooch for another the theft might not have been discovered for years,' Signora Botelli said. 'And by then no one could have suspected Claudia Medina.'

'They don't suspect her now,' Erica said bitterly. 'Claudia has convinced herself that once she has discredited me Filippo will turn to her.'

'The Conte will not go on doubting you. When he has had a chance to think clearly he will—'

'You didn't see his face yesterday . . . the way he wouldn't look at me.'

'You are misjudging him.'

'Am I?' Erica whispered, and glancing over the Signora's shoulder saw a tall dark-haired man and a petite, curvaceous woman beside him. 'I don't think so,' she added, and stepped behind the counter as Filippo ushered Claudia into the shop.

Had her misery not been so strong, Erica could almost have laughed at the look of astonishment on Signora Botelli's face. The small mouth opened in surprise and the double chins trembled, making the woman look like an agitated hen.

'C-Conte Rosetti,' she stammered. 'Wh-what can I do for you?'

'We have come to look at the designs Erica has prepared for Signora Medina.'

Signora Botelli's astonishment increased and she flung Erica a look as though warning her to say nothing. But had her life depended on it, Erica could not have spoken, for Filippo's effrontery in coming here with Claudia had rendered her speechless. He was now asking to see her jewellery designs even though he believed she had stolen his emerald. Worse still, less than seventy-two hours ago he had professed undying love for her, but now he had his arm resting delicately on Claudia's, his eyes looking at her with warmth. Fury engulfed her and it took all her will power not to lash out at him, either physically or verbally.

'I am surprised you wish to utilize my services,' she said coolly. 'You surely don't expect me to forget what happened last night?'

'I am the one who should have the most difficulty in forgetting,' Filippo retorted, and kept his voice low, as if unwilling for Signora Botelli to hear.

'You needn't whisper,' Erica said loudly. 'I have told Signora Botelli about the stolen emerald and *she* believes I'm innocent.'

Claudia Medina laughed, the first sound she had uttered since she had come into the shop.

Erica fixed her with a cold stare. 'You find that difficult to believe?'

'Not difficult, Miss Rayburn. Impossible.'

Erica's control began to slip and blindly she turned towards the office. 'Please let Signora Botelli serve you,' she said raggedly.

'We want to see your designs.' Filippo's voice caught her back. 'Please show them to us.'

'No!' she cried. 'I can't work for you or Signora Medina. You can't expect me to.'

'Please get the designs,' he repeated, and blindly she plunged into the office and bent to the drawer.

She rummaged in the bottom one and then returned to the shop with the drawings in her hand. 'I have no intention of making them,' her voice was so soft that she could hardly hear it herself, but she knew Filippo had heard, for the look he flung her was unexpectedly compassionate. Her heart began to pound and she closed her eyes and looked away.

'Please give the drawings to Signora Medina,' he said quietly. 'If she likes them as much today as she did yesterday, then—'

'I won't make them up,' Erica repeated. 'I'm leaving Venice anyway. Unless you are going to have me arrested?'

'Filippo doesn't want the publicity.'

Claudia spoke before he could do so, and Erica was surprised he should allow any woman to answer for him. Yet perhaps he had finally decided that Claudia wasn't any woman, but the special one. It was incredible to think he could change his allegiance so quickly, and she prayed they would leave the shop before her control gave way and she shamed herself by bursting into tears.

'I don't think I like the designs after all,' Claudia said.

'Not even the bracelet?' Filippo pointed to the sketch. 'Look at it again, Claudia. Pick it up and take it to the light.'

With a shrug Claudia did so, stiffening perceptibly as she saw the dapper figure of the inspector of police standing in the arcade. At once Filippo went to the door and opened it. 'Just in time, Vittorio,' he called.

The Inspector nodded, entered the shop and took the sketch from Claudia. He held one corner of it only, then carefully took a plastic bag from his jacket pocket, blew into it and dropped the sketch inside.

'What are you doing?' Claudia asked.

'I do not wish to obliterate your fingerprints, *signora*.'

'*My what?*'

'Your fingerprints. We wish to compare them with the one we found on the emerald.'

Claudia looked at the Inspector as though he were mad. 'Do you know what you are saying?' she demanded.

'Indeed I do. I am saying it would be in your best interests to make no comment on my actions for fear of implicating yourself further.'

Claudia swung round to Filippo. 'What's all this about? Do you know what this – this policeman is doing?'

'Yes, I do. He is following my suggestion.'

Only then did Claudia show genuine horror and, seeing the look on her face, Filippo's own grew unexpectedly sad.

'You are a foolish woman, Claudia. Not just wicked but foolish. Did you honestly think you could make me believe Erica was a thief?'

'There is no question of thinking it,' Claudia said haughtily. 'You had the proof given to you last night when you found the emerald in her apartment. You told me so yourself, or was that a lie?'

'You know it wasn't a lie, Claudia, because you put it there!'

Claudia flung back her head and laughed. 'Have you taken leave of your senses, Filippo? Why should I wish to do a thing like that?'

'You do not need *me* to give you your reasons.'

She went on smiling. 'I suppose the next thing you are going to say is that you found my fingerprints on the jewel box?'

'We didn't,' he replied, 'because you wore gloves. But you didn't wear gloves when you substituted the false emerald for the real one when you came to the shop.'

Claudia's eyes were two liquid pools of reproach. 'If I didn't know you better, Filippo, I would be angry with you. As it is, I am sad because you have obviously allowed your infatuation for this English girl to blind you to the truth.'

'My *love* for Erica,' he stressed the word 'love', 'has shown me the truth. I *know* she cannot be guilty, and since you were the only other person who had the opportunity of stealing the emerald—'

'What about Signora Botelli?' Claudia interrupted angrily. 'Do you love her so much that you assume her innocent too?'

'Her fingerprints weren't found on the emerald. But yours were.'

'What's so surprising about that?' Claudia demanded. 'I picked up the brooch when you showed it to me at the Palazzo weeks ago. Why shouldn't my fingerprints be on it?'

'Because when I gave Erica the brooch to repair I wiped it carefully with my handkerchief.' He glanced at Vittorio. 'All the jewellery was photographed for insurance purposes and in order to lessen the glare from the platinum and gold it was brushed with powder. The pieces were cleaned again after the photographs were taken, but the emerald brooch still had the traces of powder on it. I noticed it when I was giving it to Erica and so I wiped it again.'

'You dusted it,' Claudia said imperiously. 'That would not have obliterated my finger marks.'

'I did more than dust it,' he stated. 'I polished it.'

'I appreciate that you are trying to prove Miss Rayburn innocent.' Claudia was angry and made no attempt to hide it. 'But I refuse to let you put the blame on me.'

'It will be easy to verify if your fingerprints were put on to the emerald before the Conte wiped it clean,' the Inspector said suddenly.

'I tell you he did not wipe it clean!' Claudia almost spat out the words. 'If he did, my fingerprints would not be on it at all.'

'Fingerprints fade with time,' the Inspector assured her, 'and if yours were done when you say they were, then our analysis will show it.'

'What do you mean?'

'The mark of your forefinger and thumb are on the emerald. The Conte maintains they were put there yesterday when you possessed yourself of the stone. However, you maintain that your fingerprints were put on it some weeks ago. Our own spectrum analysis will show us who is speaking the truth.'

'Your what analysis?' Claudia demanded.

'Spectrum,' said the Inspector. 'It is a method by which the date of a fingerprint can be given almost to the hour.'

'So you have nothing to worry about, Claudia,' Filippo said quietly. 'If I have misjudged you I will repay you handsomely for having doubted you.'

'And if you have not misjudged the Signora, then you will keep your promise to us, Conte, and press charges?'

'Of course, Inspector. I have given you my word on that.'

'What word?' Claudia demanded.

'We had to have the spectrum machine flown here from Naples,' the Inspector replied. 'We refused to go to the expense unless the Conte promised to press charges if you were found to be guilty.'

Erica turned away, not wishing to hear the next outburst

from Claudia. But there was silence and only as it length-
ened did she turn round. Claudia was still by the window,
looking from Filippo to the Inspector and then back to
Filippo again.

'I don't understand what game you are playing,' she said
in a shaky voice.

'It is no game, Claudia,' Filippo replied. 'Under normal
circumstances I would not have given Vittorio my promise
to prosecute. You know how much I hate publicity. I would
even prefer to let a thief escape – providing I had my jewels
back – than have the notoriety of a court case. But where the
name of the woman I love is at stake, then I have no
choice.'

'Her name isn't at stake! No one knows what happened
last night.'

'Vittorio knows, Signora Botelli knows and *you* know.
And *you*, I am sure, would see that all our friends knew too.
Because of that it was not enough for *me* to believe in
Erica's innocence; I had to prove it for everyone else to
know. And that meant finding the real culprit.'

'It hurts me to think you should have suspected me,'
Claudia said sadly. 'I thought we were fond of each
other.'

'I *was* fond of you, Claudia, but I *love* Erica.'

'Erica!' Claudia spat out the word. 'Erica, Erica. I'm sick
of that name. Is that all you can think about – that pale-
faced fool with the big innocent eyes! You're mad to be in
love with her. She will bore you to death in six months and
in a year you will be running around with other women!'

'Be quiet!' Filippo thundered.

'Please, my friend,' the Inspector said. 'We are digressing
from the point. I suggest you and Signora Medina come to
police headquarters while we do this analysis.'

'So that you can arrest me?' Claudia gave a cry and tried
to push past the Inspector to throw herself against Filippo.
'Will your conscience let you send me to prison? The
widow of your greatest friend – the man you loved as a
brother!'

'I will destroy anyone who threatened to destroy Erica.' Filippo almost snarled the words. 'And you haven't even got the courage to admit your guilt. If you force me to prove it I'll —'

'I don't care about your proof!' Claudia screamed. 'And I don't care about you! If you can love a stupid little nothing, then you deserve her!' The dark eyes were no longer limpid, but flashing with fire. 'I should never have put the emerald in her apartment. If you hadn't found it you would never have been able to prove it was me.'

Filippo fell back a step. The anger had gone from his face, and blanched of all colour and emotion it looked like a mask.

'You could have got away with it,' he muttered. 'You could have had a million lire if you had been content with money rather than destroying Erica.'

'Destroying her was worth more to me than the money,' Claudia said, and she was bereft of emotion too. All anger had drained from her and she stood in front of them as devoid of feeling as a zombie. 'You were mine, Filippo, and I wasn't going to let any other woman have you. Being your wife meant more to me than a hundred emeralds!'

'Indeed it would,' he said quietly.

'Not because of the money,' she said. 'But because I wanted you. *You*.' She put out her hands in a blind gesture and the Inspector caught hold of them and led her to the door.

'Take her home,' Filippo said harshly. 'Then sit with her while she packs and leaves Venice.'

Only then did Claudia appear to hear what was said, for she turned and looked at Filippo. 'You are letting me go?'

'Yes. As you just said, you are the widow of the man who was my closest friend. It is for his sake that I am doing it, not yours. But you are to leave Italy for the next five years, and even when you return, you are not to live in Venice nor to mix in my circle of friends.' He looked at the Inspector. 'I suggest you take a statement from Signora Medina and put it on record. If she does not keep her side of the bargain I am sure you will always be able to find the file again.'

'We never close a case,' Vittorio agreed, and held open the door for Claudia to step through it. She did so and the Inspector glanced over his shoulder at Erica. 'I hope we meet again under more pleasant circumstances, Miss Rayburn.'

Erica nodded, but was too overcome to speak. She searched round wildly for somewhere to sit, afraid that she was going to faint. Strong hands came around her and she was half lifted into the office. The door was closed and she was alone with Filippo at last.

'Forgive me for what I did, *cara mia*,' he pleaded. 'But I dared not tell you what was in my mind last night for fear you would give yourself away when I came in here with Claudia this morning.'

'You mean you – you were planning it *then*?'

'Of course. I knew you had not taken the emerald.'

'You never said so.' Tears poured down her cheeks, but she didn't wipe them away and he came over and, taking his handkerchief from his pocket, did so for her.

'Did I need to say it?' he asked. 'Didn't you know I could never doubt you any more than you could ever doubt me?'

'Oh, Filippo,' she cried, 'I've been so blind!'

'You have always been blind about me. That's why we will be married quickly. Only when you are truly mine will you have sufficient confidence in yourself to realize how much I love you.'

She leaned against him and felt his arms come around her. His heart was hammering and she pressed close to his chest, hearing in the fast beat the echo of her own and knowing that for him too this last dreadful scene had been a taxing one. 'It was clever of you to suspect, Claudia.'

'Didn't *you*?'

'Yes,' she admitted. 'I nearly came to tell you last night, but I was afraid you wouldn't believe me.'

'I would have been furious with you if you had left your apartment. I told you not to do so.'

She glanced up at him. 'You were very insistent about

that, Filippo. Why?'

He hesitated and for the first time she saw genuine fear in his eyes. 'I had a feeling Claudia might harm you; that she might realize my love for you would make me want to marry you regardless of what you had done.'

Erica moistened lips that had suddenly gone dry. 'You thought she might have killed me?'

He nodded. 'I had one of the servants stand outside your apartment all night and watch you until you were safely in the shop this morning.'

His words made her tremble and she burrowed against him. 'You would never have been able to prove it was Claudia without that new fingerprint analysis.'

'Indeed not.'

'Then there'd have been no way of establishing my innocence.'

'Indeed not.'

'I can't believe it,' she went on, and tilted her head to look into his face.

'Indeed not,' he said again. 'You would be exceedingly simple if you did.'

She looked up and saw the twinkle in his eyes and the laughter which, bubbling within him, made his shoulders shake.

'What are you saying, Filippo?'

'That the whole thing was a lie, my darling. A great whopping lie which my brilliant friend, Vittorio, dreamed up.'

'You mean you can't tell the age of a fingerprint?'

'Neither the age nor the sex. It is possible to tell the age of many other things, as I'm sure your father knows. Pottery, metal, bones, trees – but fingerprints and women keep their age to themselves!'

Erica started to laugh, but the laughter changed swiftly to tears and she turned her face into Filippo's shoulder and wept.

'Have a good cry,' he said tenderly. 'It will make you feel better.'

'I feel better already,' she gulped. 'I'm so happy, Filippo. This morning when I woke up I thought my life was over.'

'It's just beginning,' he whispered, and placed his mouth gently upon hers. 'I don't think we will have that big engagement party after all. We'll fly to London today to see your father and make arrangements there for a special licence. How long will that take?'

'Three days, but—'

'As long as that?' he protested.

'Filippo!' she cried.

'Erica,' he said softly, and with his lips on hers gave her no chance to protest any more.

Harlequin Collection Editions

Please note: The number in brackets indicates the original Harlequin Romance number.

Harlequin Collection Editions

Please note: The number in brackets indicates the original Harlequin Romance number.

Harlequin Collection Editions

Please note: The number in brackets indicates the original Harlequin Romance number.

Harlequin Collection Editions

Please note: The number in brackets indicates the original Harlequin Romance number.

Complete and mail this coupon today!